The Magic of Simon Tombs

John L. French

PADWOLF PUBLISHING INC.
WWW.PADWOLF.COM
www.facebook.com/Padwolf

THE MAGIC OF SIMION TOMBS
© 2019 John L. French

cover by Warren Design

ISBN 10 digit 1-890096-90-3   ISBN 13 digit 978-1-890096-90-8
Printed in the USA First Printing

To my friend and co-worker
Pamela K. Shaw

CONTENTS

FREELY CHOSEN

A neighborhood fair. One tent has a sign – "Free Henna Tattoos & Face Painting." Inside is a cheerful young woman turning a young boy into a pirate. Behind her are examples of her work. For the kids, there are movie, comic, and cartoon characters. For teens and adults, she offers a selection of intricate geometric patterns. There's a line outside the tent.

"Is this really free?" one mother asks.

"Yes, but offerings are always welcome." The young woman indicates a tip jar.

"Are these only for kids?"

She shakes her head. "No age limit. Any design on anyone – anywhere you like." She looks toward a privacy screen in the back of the tent. "Anywhere."

The mother smiles. She comes back later and leaves with a surprise for her husband.

Tips fill the jar. Business is good. Mostly kids in the morning, teens and adults later in the day. While some of these pick comic or movie art, most get a design – on their face, on their arm, around their wrist. Some go behind the screen.

The end of the day. The young woman is exhausted. *Hard work,* she thinks, *but ultimately worth it.* She folds her tent. Next week – same thing, different place.

The face paint washes off. The henna-like dye seems to fade. Unless one took a photo no trace seems to remain.

Comes a certain night, a ritual is begun, a Power are invoked. Where the now forgotten tattoos were comes a sickly green glow. Some see it and worry and wonder. Some kids think it cool. Others sleep through it. These last are the lucky ones.

In the morning after a certain night come the screams as the husks of teens, mothers, boyfriends, and children are discovered.

In the morning after a certain night, as a city starts to panic, a young woman smiles. She has been and will be young for many, many years. Her youth and beauty renewed; her masters well fed by the sacrifice of those who choose the runes, offered their bodies, and willingly gave tribute.

A Bargain Well Made

Simon Tombs was on his second drink when the woman fell through the door. It was obvious to everyone in Sebastian's that she was hurt but only Simon was aware that she had been assaulted in the most brutal of ways then dumped from a moving car. It was his nature to know these things, just as it was his nature to do something about them.

"Call 9-1-1," he shouted, expecting at least one of the staff to follow his order. He then ran to the woman. Unmindful of the blood leaking from her head onto his clothing, he held a cloth against her open wound as he whispered the spell that would cause it to begin healing.

He did not ask her what had happened. Her blood told him most of what he needed to know – an attack in a parking garage, the assailant forcing her into a car then, in the darkness of the garage, beating and violating her. He drives off with her moaning and bleeding on the passenger seat, possibly saving her for later. When they hit the street, she somehow works the door, opens it, and flings herself to the pavement. Then she finds Sebastian's – and him.

Simon cradled the woman as she moaned and cried and mentally relived every second of the worse moments of her life. Other than the bruising, her head wound, and severe road rash he sensed no other physical damage, no, the occipital bone beneath her left eye was broken.

He was singing the woman a calming song when the sirens stopped in front of the bar. Several uniformed men and women then crashed in. One of them gently took the woman from Simon's arms after which two others not so gently braced him against the front wall.

"You've got blood on you," said a cop whose name tag identified him as "J. Nolan."

"Very observant," Simon said calmly. "Now would you like to

guess my age and weight?"

What Nolan was about to do next was obvious to all. Simon was already planning the slight shift that would have resulted in the cop hitting his partner in the back of the head. All this was forestalled when the bartender cried out, "He didn't do it, you morons. He was helping the poor girl," at the same time a woman with stripes on her sleeves shouted,

"Stand down, Junior."

As Junior Nolan backed away from Simon the sergeant approached.

"Your name, Sir?"

No apology. Simon had not expected one. He had dealt with police before, both in Baltimore and many other cities and countries.

Dutifully he identified himself and displayed the required driver's license both to prove his identity and provide his current address. When asked, he even gave the sergeant his cell phone number, one of them at least.

"Simon Tombs. Where have I heard that name before?" The sergeant, whose name tag ID'd her as "B. Marsh" wondered.

"I know, Sarge," said the cop who had almost been hit in the back of the head. "This guy's had a few run-ins with Hood in Homicide."

Sergeant Marsh now looked at Simon suspiciously. "Is that so?"

Simon nodded. "Caitlin and I have met. I was a 'person of interest' in some of her cases."

"And how did that turn out?"

"She lost interest."

Normally Simon would have said this with a smile that dared his interrogator to proceed further and at her own risk. But given the events of the day, he kept a straight face and any challenges to himself.

More sirens announced the arrival of an ambulance for the woman and of plainclothes detectives. Very plain, Simon noted.

After Sergeant Marsh explained the situation to them, one of the detectives, an older man whose face told the world that he had seen far too much and had spent too much time dealing with what he had seen to be worried about anything as minor as pleasantries or courtesy, walked up to Simon.

"Any of that your blood?" he asked.

"Not a drop."

"Well, we'll need ..."

Before the detective could finish his "request," Simon had stripped off his suit coat, tie, and shirt and had handed them to Officer Nolan. "Take care of this, would you please, Junior."

Standing in suit pants and t-shirt, his muscular arms on view for those enjoyed such sights, Simon held himself as if he were still the best-dressed person in the room.

"Anything else, Detective Payne?" Without waiting for an answer he went on. "If so, Sergeant Brenda knows how to reach me. Now if you'll excuse me, I'd like to finish my drink."

And so he did, picking up his drink and moving to a back table while the BPD worked the scene at the front door.

It was not until the officers and detectives were back at the Sex Offense Unit that they wondered how this Tombs fellow knew Sergeant Marsh's first name was Brenda or how he knew Detective Payne's name at all.

"I'm looking for Heather Paul. What room is she in?"

The charge nurse looked up at Simon in surprise. She hadn't seen him come on to the floor.

"I'm sorry," she said automatically, her voice managing to convey both her authority as gatekeeper and her regret that Simon had wasted a trip, "but Ms. Paul is not allowed visitors."

"My name is Simon Tombs. I'm the exception that proves the rule. Ms. Paul asked me to visit."

Actually, it was Megan from Sebastian's who had asked him. Not knowing his name, Heather had called the bar and asked that her message be passed on.

"But the police ..."

"Aren't here. And unless Ms. Paul is under arrest they have no authority over her, you, or even me." *Especially me*, Simon thought. "Now, which is her room?"

Simon said this last with a smile, but there was something in his blue-gray eyes that suggested to the nurse that it would be best to do what this man requested.

"Room 739. It's to your left and down the hall."

"Thank you."

When Simon walked in the room he right away noticed that Heather Paul looked much better than she had when he held her in his arms while they waited for the police to arrive. Better physically, that is. There was a hunted look in her eyes that told him that she relived her trauma over and over and probably needed medication to help her sleep.

Would that life were simple and that its worse pain came from stubbing one's toe, he thought. To the woman sitting up in the bed, he said,

"Ms. Paul, I'm ..."

"You're the man who helped me after I ... on that day."

For Heather Paul it would always be "that day."

"I only did what anyone would have done."

"No, Mr. Tombs, you did more. I felt it. The doctors say that I'm healing faster than anyone should with my injuries. While you were holding me, you ... did something. You have powers. You're a healer, aren't you?"

"Among other things," he admitted.

"But you can't fix everything, can you?"

"No," he said with as much compassion as he could.

"It's like he took a piece of my soul away. A piece that will never grow back. Does that make sense?"

More than you know, Simon said to himself. To Heather he said only, "Yes."

"Mr. Tombs, I have no right to ask this of you, and at least two police detectives have warned me about having to do with you, but is there any way... you can make me whole again?"

Simon had suffered for his magic, suffered because of it. There was a price for what he did, what he was. Usually, he made others pay, but there were times when he had to pick up the check.

Did this woman know what she was asking? Would she be

willing to risk more of her soul to get back its missing piece?

"Ms. Paul, Heather, if I may. I can't undo what's been done. And I cannot give you back what you have lost. Just as I could not mend your injuries, only help them to heal."

"Then can you help the rest of me to heal?"

Looking into her haunted eyes he saw the strength hidden behind them. *Maybe she is strong enough*, he decided.

"Not here. Not now," he said, "but when you get home, you will find a small, glass dropper bottle containing a clear liquid. If your suffering becomes too much for you, add one drop to a glass of water. Then the memory of what you have suffered will fade into something like a dream. You will recall it, but it will not seem real. Two drops will make the memory go away completely. You will not even know that you have forgotten it."

"And three drops, Simon?'

Three or more drops was the risk, the chance, the price of the magic.

"Three or more drops will make Heather Paul go away completely. Your whole self, and not just a piece of it, will be gone forever."

"I ... I understand," she said and Simon believed that she did.

"That Detective Hood. She said that the police have some leads. I suppose I should wait until after the trial to do anything." She shuddered at that thought. "I don't know if I could face him in court."

"I wouldn't worry about that, Heather."

Like calls to like. That is the basis of most soft magic. The connection between one thing and another, and those things with the universe. Scientists explained it through something called quantum mechanics. Magic by a different name.

After the police had left Sebastian's and Simon had finished his drink, he noticed that he still had some of the woman's blood on him. It had dripped on his hand, and some had been transferred to his face as he held her. Plus it had stained his offered handkerchief when she had used it to wipe tears from her face.

Tears and blood. It was enough, especially the tears, considering why they had been shed.

At his quiet table in the back of the bar, Simon closed his eyes and concentrated. Concentrated on her blood, on her tears, and on the feelings he had received from her when he lent her his healing power. Soon he knew her. Knew that her name was Heather Paul. Knew where she lived, where she worked, and where she had parked her car.

The garage was far enough away from Sebastian's that the police might not find it before he did. Might. Not wishing to be found at the scene of a crime – again – Simon had little time to waste. But first, he had to stop at his apartment.

Dressed in a new suit, Simon walked the dark ramps of the Holiday Garage. Poor lighting, no cameras, a movie director's dream set for the "something bad is about to happen" scene. Still, it was cheap and within walking distance of the downtown offices.

The physic residue of the attack still lingered, drawing him toward it. Simon felt what had happened – how he grabbed her, forced her into the car, forced himself on her, beat her because she had dared scream and fight back.

She had bled in that car. His car. He had bled as well. Simon delved deep into himself, expended his power, demanded that the universe connect the blood in the car with that still on his hand. As it most times did, the universe consented, displaying to his mind's eye just where the car was, the blood on his hand burning away as a reminder of the cost of magic.

Simon left the garage and caught a City Circulator bus north to Charles Village. He found the car at 31st and Calvert Streets, two blocks east of the bus stop, just outside a residential apartment tower.

As he did with many things in his world, Simon had a way with doors and locks. He was able to quickly open the car and slide in without anyone noticing him doing so. After that, no magic was needed for him to check the car's registration for the owner's name and address.

Simon smiled when he saw that his quarry lived in the tower

apartment. His smile widened when he read that the apartment was on the twelfth floor.

Simon's knock was answered promptly. "Mr. Jukes? Mr. Derrick Jukes?"

"Yeah. Who the hell are you?"

"Mind if I come in?" And without waiting for a reply Simon brushed past the larger man into a very untidy living room.

Interrupting Jukes's "What the hell?" Simon said,

"In answer to your first question, Mr. Jukes, I am justice. I am vengeance. But you can call me Simon."

As he spoke, Simon assessed his prey. He was larger than Simon and possibly stronger. But he appeared to be a brute, one who would fight with little or no finesse. Not that that mattered. Simon had no intention of fighting him, not unless Jukes insisted. In which case the end would only come that much sooner and would be much less satisfying.

There was blood on Jukes's clothing, Heather Paul's, judging by how the mark on Simon's hand where her blood had been started burning again. But Jukes was saying something.

"I asked if you were a cop."

Simon ignored him. "How many, Mr. Jukes? How many other women other than the one today have you beaten and brutalized?'

"Cop or not, I don't have to tell you a thing."

"No, you don't. You've told me enough."

Jukes's body language had replied to Simon's question. There had been others. Just how many may have mattered to his victims, and to the police, but not to Simon and soon, not to Jukes himself.

"And to ease your mind, Mr. Jukes, I'm not a cop. Just a private citizen with a warning."

Jukes was clearly becoming irritated with this stranger who had invaded his home. He had positioned himself so as to be able to throw Simon through the still open door but he had to ask,

"What kind of warning?'

"A final one, Mr. Jukes. Get your affairs in order. If you have any loved ones say your farewells."

"So you're saying the cops are coming?'

"Oh, they'll be here eventually. They'll fit Part A into Part B and soon put the puzzle together. And it will have your face on it. Whether you're here to meet them when they come," Simon sighed dramatically, "that's up to the fates. Goodbye, Mr. Jukes."

A clearly confused Derrick Jukes took the offered hand. But before he could think of an appropriate reply, whether verbal or physical, Simon was out the open door and down the stairs.

I have you now, Simon thought, studying his right hand as he rose the City Circulator back downtown and to where his car was parked. He'd soon be back in his own apartment. Then it would be time for some darker magic.

"No, I wouldn't worry about testifying, Heather, or even having to see your assailant again. Something tells me that the case will soon be closed."

As if on cue, the door to Heather Paul's hospital room opened and Homicide Detective Caitlin Hood walked in.

"Tombs, what are you doing here?"

"Visiting a friend. Right, Heather?"

"Yes, Simon," the woman in the bed replied.

"Ms. Paul, you don't know who, or what, this man is."

There was a touch of anger in Heather's voice as she replied, "I know that he's someone who comforted me, and who's come to visit me and help me recover. Now what do you want, Detective?"

"I think it's me that Caitlin wants. If you'll excuse us?"

Once the mage and the detective were in a borrowed consultation room he said, "Let me guess, the charge nurse called you."

"She had orders. We expected that you'd show up."

"Very good, Caitlin. You're getting very good at this detective business."

Ignoring Simon's barbs and his constant use of her first name, Hood asked,

"Derrick Jukes, know him?"

Simon shook his head. "Should I?"

"You tell me. He's on a slab at the Medical Examiner's Office.

In our search of his apartment we found items belonging to Ms. Paul. I'm sure that when his DNA is compared to the evidence left by her assailant it will be a match. Now, where were you yesterday afternoon?"

"All afternoon?"

"Why not?"

Simon told her. She believed him but didn't want to; didn't want to believe that when Derrick Jukes met his end Simon Tombs was having lunch with two city councilmen, a rabbi, and a Roman Catholic bishop.

"The councilmen are both lay ministers at their churches. We meet once a month to discuss and compare religious beliefs. That is, they discuss and I compare."

"I don't like it when you're involved in my cases, Tombs."

"But you do love multiple clearances, don't you, Caitlin?'

The detective's hopes, which Simon had just dashed, suddenly rose. "What makes you suspect that there will be multiple clearances?"

"Just that it's likely that this Jukes has done to other women what he did to Ms. Paul," is what his mouth said to the detective. However, his eyes and his smile told her much, much more.

"And if I asked, I suspect you could tell me just who those other women are."

"But you won't, Caitlin, because then you'd have to ask how I know. And you're not quite ready."

"For what?"

Simon's smile faded and his blue-grey eyes became serious. "The Truth, Detective Hood."

Tombs was right, Hood realized, she wasn't ready. She had vague suspicions but had never followed up on them. Better the world she knew than the one Tombs might live in.

The detective rose. "I'm leaving. Say my goodbyes to Ms. Paul. You can tell her that the case against her assailant has been abated by death."

"And that justice has been done?"

"If you like. And, Tombs, stay away from my cases, and stop

calling me Caitlin."

"As to the first, I'll do my best. As for the second, agreed …
Katie."

Detective Hood left without a word, leaving Simon alone with
his thoughts.

The handshake. The willing contact between Jukes and him.
The established connection that allowed Simon to work his magic.
To send the compulsion.

What must it have been like for Derrick Jukes, unable to leave
his apartment on the last day of his life? Approaching his door but
not capable of opening it. Was it then that he felt his control over his
life fading away? Did he have lunch, a satisfying last meal? Or did
he pace like the trapped animal he was?

And when Simon and his discussion group, a group he had long
ago put together for occasions such as this, had begun to enjoy their
own lunch, how did Jukes feel when his body walked over to the
window and opened the lower sash? Did his feelings of helplessness
come close to those he attacked? Or did that moment come as he
plunged out of the window to his death twelve floors below?

Not quite fair, one might think. A few terrible moments for
Jukes, a lifetime of them for his victims. Still, there was the afterlife,
Simon reflected, and unless Jukes was able to make his peace on the
way down, his suffering was only beginning.

The smile returned to Simon's face. It was time to tell Heather
Paul that justice had been done. And whatever the price was for
Jukes he'd willingly pay it and consider it a bargain well made.

All In

The eyes appeared first. Red predator eyes shining from the shadows. Then came the teeth. Sharp daggers, designed for ripping and tearing. Only then did the creature speak to him, addressing him by a name he had almost forgotten.

Simon Tombs was not disturbed that a creature of the Deep Pit had seemingly manifested in his bedroom. It had happened before. He knew the appearance for what it was, a sending only. Beings such as this were too damned to ever escape their punishment and had to work their evil through lesser demons or human agents and fools.

Simon was none of those. While it was true that he had knowledge of things most people did not believe and put this knowledge to use when he thought it best, he was, mostly, on the side of the saints and angels. Still, he had had dealings with the dark ones in the past and had, so far, come away with only minor stains on his soul.

No, it was not the Pit creature that disturbed Simon. It was the fact that it had chosen to speak in a voice that combined the best qualities of Betty Boop, Jessica Rabbit, and Jane Jetson. It was quite a seductive voice.

Still, it would not do to let on just how much he was discomforted by it.

"I thought," he said to the Hellish shade, his own voice a touch of menace mixed with irritation, "I told you never to call me here."

"I have need of you." The voice now was Jeannie, Samantha Stevens, and Morticia Addams. This thing knew him.

And he knew it. It was not merely a denizen of the Deep Pit. It was one of its masters. One of the few that mankind knew by the collective name of Satan. One of the traitors to Heaven who had been cast out just after Creation began.

"You have no claim or power over me," he told it. "Rather the contrary I should think. I've read the Book. I know the Names."

The Book. The Names. Names from a time when Eden was still a fresh memory. Names that had tempted mankind into its own Fall. Names inscribed in one of the first books ever written. The true names of the Fallen. Names of Power.

Simon had read the Book. It had been copied and recopied ad infinitum from the stone tablet on which the story and names had first been carved. It was guarded by a single monk who dwelt in a small cave on the edge of the Land between the lands, the one said to be guarded by a fiery sword.

Simon and eleven others had mounted an expedition to find this Land. Despite the monk's warning, they had crossed over, slipping from our reality into another, a bleak arid world with no Sword and no Garden. One which had not known the tread of man for countless millennia.

Only two made it back, Simon and one other, and that other was not quite sane. He ran off, leaving Simon behind.

Simon stayed with and learned from monk for several weeks. It was during these weeks that he was shown the Book and taught how to pronounce the Names.

"They walk among us in the guise of men," the monk had told him. "It is best that there are those who know how to stop them."

Names hold power over the beings they describe. Which is why Simon changed his every few decades or so.

The true names of demons and devils. He did not know how much more pain they could cause those damned to Hell but he did know they could be used to command them or forestall their plans. It was a responsibility that Simon did not take lightly. It was one he tried not to think of at all.

"I know the names," Simon repeated and the creature grew smaller, shrinking back into the shadows. "Do not think to command me. Why have you come to me?"

This time the Fallen spoke in the voices of several actors who had played secret agents in the 1960's and 1970's.

"There is one bargaining with humans, a mid-circle demon who walks among your kind. He seeks to become more powerful."

Simon shrugged. "I can't and won't stop fools who think to barter away the most precious thing they have. We are each free to choose our own salvation or damnation."

"Orthon cares not for souls. He cares only for the empty shells left behind. He seeks to fill them."

"So why tell me, or anyone for that matter? I would think you would be pleased."

"There is no pleasure in Perdition, save that found in the suffering of others. Call it what you will – envy, spite, the stopping of a possible threat to our mastery. For masters we are, and we would not be slaves again."

"And that attitude is why you're still in Hell."

After giving out this unwanted and unheeded bit of advice, Simon asked,

"Where can I find this Orthon?"

"In this city, in the house of luck."

Simon nodded in understanding. "Thank you. You can go now," he said in dismissal.

"Must I? Here there is less pain. Allow me to stay and I will give you …"

"*Apage Satanas*," said Simon in his best school-boy Latin. "*Redire ad Perditionem.*"

Thus commanded, the creature's voice fell silent and the eyes closed. The teeth, however, remained for several minutes, a Cheshire threat in the darkness.

After the Pit Lord had departed, Simon thoroughly checked his apartment for any lingering traces it may have left behind. He found none, not that he had expected to. Even minor demons know enough not to leave behind anything with which a skilled practitioner can work a compulsive summoning. Then he did some research.

Orthon, Possessor of Bodies, using them to walk the mortal plane. Since they were, in a sense, loaners, he did not take very good care of them, resulting in him needing a near endless supply. Running out meant a return to the Pit and conflict with his fellow demons, especially Abdiel, the self-styled Lord of Slaves.

Unfortunately, there were fools aplenty, always willing to make a deal or summon him back while seeking an easy way to get what they think they wanted or needed. As Simon had said earlier, those who knowingly entered into an infernal compact got what they deserved. But from what his visitor had told him, it was possible that Orthon's latest targets were not that knowing.

Fortuna's was a restaurant in Baltimore's Fells Point. It was located just off Broadway and chances are you would walk past it unless you were actively searching for it. The food was good, the wine passable, and the beer bottled or on tap, whichever you preferred. And for those in the know, there was a back stairway that led to a second-floor room where there was almost always a card game in progress.

The type of games played varied according to fashion and the whims of the players. There was room enough for several games to be played at once – poker, blackjack, acey-deucy, and, of course, Texas Hold'em. If the game could be played with a standard deck of playing cards it could be played at Fortuna's. It was rumored that some years ago five thousand dollars changed hands during a particularly intense game of Old Maid.

The rules within Fortuna's card room were simple – cash only on the table, checks and IOU's allowed if the two parties agreed. No alcohol, no drugs, no weapons, and no cheating. The breaking of the first three might sometimes be forgiven, but breaking the last was an unpardonable offense. No one was ever quite sure what had become of those who had tried, but all were certain that the offenders had never been seen again.

Simon knew of Fortuna's and played there occasionally. He played mostly for recreation, making sure not to win or lose so much so as to attract attention. And he never used his magic. That would have been cheating.

"Please ask Momma to have a drink with me," Simon asked his waiter after he's finished his meal of some kind of meat in white gravy over rice. "Tell her it's Simon," he added as the waiter was about to object that Momma Fortuna did not drink with the customers.

Simon could never decide whether Momma was Italian with a trace of Spanish or the other way around. Whatever she was, she encompassed the very best of both countries. She was a largish woman, with dark hair that threatened to go gray but somehow never did. Almost always pleasant, except when she had to restore order in the upstairs room, she greeted Simon as if he were a favored cousin, or a former lover, or possibly both.

"Simon," she said when they'd both sat down after the mandatory smothering hug, "You never change, you never seem to get older."

"And Momma, you grow more beautiful every time I see you."

"Flatterer. I'm sure you use that line on every woman you meet."

"True, but with you I mean it. You are so full of inner beauty that it cannot help but spill out for all to see."

"And you, Simon, are full of something else. Now, what trouble brings you here?"

"Momma, can't I just come here to have a nice time."

"You can and you do. And unlike the others who climb the back stairs, you always have a meal. And you tip your waiter enough that I don't have to pay him that night. But you were here three weeks ago and by now I know your habits." Momma Fortuna looked in the direction of the back stairs. "It's the new player, isn't it?"

"Which new player is that?"

"The one with much money and even more luck. He is here every third or fourth night. He always wins, and almost always leaves with some poor fool's paper in his pocket."

"Do you think he's cheating?"

Momma shook her head. "If he is he's the best I've seen, and I've seen them all, both here in Baltimore and, well, elsewhere."

Momma did not speak of her past. Simon liked to think it was adventurous, scandalous, and involved the ruin of many men and maybe a few women.

"Any objections to my checking things out?"

Momma smiled and shook her head. "I was hoping that was why you'd come. But remember, Simon, even you have to follow the rules."

"Not generally, Momma, but for you, always."

Orthon was not hard to spot. He was sitting at the furthest table from the door, his back to the wall. To the average person, he would have smelled slightly of stale cigarette smoke and the need to shower more often. Simon, however, detected a whiff of brimstone and the faint stench of the Pit.

Orthon looked like a mid-level office worker, one who put in his eight to ten hours, went home, ate, then spent the rest of the night watching whatever was on television, not caring exactly what that was. Simon wondered what the former owner of the body had wanted so badly to have fallen for whatever line Orthon had fed him. No wedding ring and no sign that there had ever been one. Maybe that's what the demon had offered, nights of passion during which his partner, probably Orthon in female form, said something like "I want your body" to which the poor fool would have replied, "It's yours."

Contract offered and accepted, and Orthon had a new body ready to go when he finished with his current one.

The demon looked up when Simon entered the room, barely glancing at him as the magician sat at a different table. Orthon would take him for just another mortal unless Simon used his magic. Not that Simon would. The night was strictly recon with no confrontation planned.

The game at Simon's table was straight draw – jacks or better, show your openers if you dropped out. Simon managed not to lose too much, a remarkable feat given that most of his attention was on what was happening at the back table. There the game was Texas Hold'em. From what Simon could tell, the demon was winning every third hand or so. Just how he was winning them Simon couldn't tell. Each of the three tables had a house dealer, which meant that the only cards Orthon handled were his own. And switching cards in a game where you didn't know what your opponents held could be fatal in this or any other poker room.

No paper was given that night, no one finding the need to bet more than what was in his pocket and so no IOUs were written. Nor were they on the next night Simon visited Momma's upstairs room.

On the third night, however …

The player to Simon's left bet heavily after the flop with all but one of the players calling him. He checked on the turn but doubled Orthon's raise when the demon made it. That was enough for everyone but Simon but even he threw his cards in when Orthon raised yet again and gambler matched it.

Simon didn't see the river card fall. Instead, he was watching Orthon. There was something – a shift of his eyes, a twitch of this mouth that may have been a suppressed smile, a slight movement of his body – that told Simon that he knew what cards his opponent held and that the demon had him beat.

"All in," the gambler said, pushing the money in front of him into the center of the table.

But this wasn't the downtown Horseshoe Casino and it wasn't Vegas. There was no buy-in, no one was playing for a bracelet, and the players did not start with an equal amount of chips. This was a cash game, and the only limit was what you had on you or in front of you.

Orthon smiled and met the bet. Then he pushed in three thousand more.

"I … I can't meet that," the gambler said, his dream of windfall winnings suddenly vanishing.

"Too bad," Orthon said, preparing to rake in his winnings. But then he stopped. "Look," he said, somewhat kindly, "I hate to win this way. Makes me feel that I'm stealing the pot. Tell you what, I've seen you around the tables before. Give me your marker for the three grand and we'll let the cards decide."

The gambler looked at the pot, then at Orthon. He checked his cards. "Okay," he said, looking around for something to write on.

"Here, just fill in the amount and sign," the demon said, offering a preprinted form the size and shape of a dollar bill.

The gambler hesitated, maybe realizing that the rat he smelled wasn't just smoke and bad hygiene but something more sinister.

"I do this for a living, friend," came the much-practiced explanation. "I like to be prepared. But I'm willing to take the pot without a showdown."

"No," the gambler said, quickly signing the paper for three thousand dollars. Handing the note over, he then turned up his cards, his pocket aces giving him a full house, aces over kings.

Orthon was no longer resisting the smile. "Not bad, but I'm afraid," he turned up pocket kings for four of a kind, "that you owe me three thousand dollars."

Watching what he had believed just a minute before were his winnings going into the pockets of someone else, the stunned gambler said, "I'm … I'm good for it."

"I know you are, one way or the other."

Simon did not hear this last. He had gathered his money and was out the door just as the two kings fell. Standing outside Fortuna's, he waited.

"Tough luck," he said as the gambler emerged. Recognizing Simon from inside, he tried a smile then, "Yeah, guess that's why they call it gambling."

Simon replied sympathetically. "We've all been there." Which was a lie. The magician had been many places but never where the gambler was or might be going.

"I'm curious," Simon added. "I know it's none of my business but how did that note read?'

The gambler never felt the little *push* that Simon used to make him want to reply.

"Just that I pledged myself to pay three thousand dollars to the holder of the note within three months."

"Myself, one word or two?" Another *push*.

"Come to think of it, there was a break, between the y and the s. A misprint I guess."

No, it's not, Simon thought, understanding part of the demon's scheme.

"Do yourself a favor," he told the gambler, "if you have to borrow the money or sell a kidney, get that money together and pay off the note as soon as you can. Then never gamble with that man again." Another push, almost a compulsion. The man would have a headache come morning but that was the price of magic.

"But why, for God's sake?"

"Not for His sake, but for your own."

Myself. My self.

Not much difference between the two. But by signing the note the gambler had backed his debt with his very being. If for any reason he failed to pay, even if he tried and Orthon had moved on, when the note came due the demon could claim his body.

That's how demons worked. That's how they trapped people – by adhering to the very letter of the agreement, interpreting it the way that benefited them the most. It didn't matter that the other party was not aware of what he was signing, or had thought he was agreeing to something else. It was *caveat emptor* and most of the time not only did the buyer fail to beware, he was not even aware of the exact terms of the agreement.

That was the easy part of the problem. All Simon had left was figuring out how Orthon was winning.

He wasn't cheating, of that Simon was sure. By sitting at one of Fortuna's tables he had tacitly agreed not to cheat and while demons of his sort may tempt, mislead, omit, and obscure, they could not renege on their own agreements.

Besides, Momma had not caught him at it, and this was a woman who had once produced a three of spades she'd hidden in her bra to fill an inside straight flush (or so the story went). She knew cheaters and all their tricks.

So if Orthon's winning was thanks to more than luck and skill, it had to be due to natural abilities. Demons had more of those than mere mortals.

Fortunately, so did Simon.

Sitting behind his desk in his study, Simon began dealing out cards. Nothing fancy, just one card at a time from the top of the desk. After the last card was turned up, he shuffled and did it again, each time extending his magic just a little bit more. After the twelfth time, he began to get a sense of what card was coming next – high/low, suit, or rank. By the twentieth deal, he could guess the card seventy percent of the time. By the thirty-fifth deal, he knew what the card would be every time.

He switched to a new deck. Despite using the same level of power his predictive accuracy dropped to twenty percent. With each deal, however, it increased. A form of sympathetic magic, Simon decided. One had to become familiar with the deck.

But would it work with the games at Fortuna's where the players didn't deal their own cards? They only handled the cards they were dealt.

That should not matter, he decided. Cards were a part of a deck. Like the cells of the body, each part held the secret of the whole. That was the theory. There was, Simon knew, only one way to test it.

Simon became a regular at Fortuna's. It was five days before Orthon came in to play. By then Simon had confirmed his theory. Play with the same deck long enough and it would be as if the cards were dealt face up.

Of course, he did not take advantage of his fellow players. Instead, he used his knowledge of their hands to make the games interesting for all, making sure that no one lost or won too much because of him.

Orthon was there when Simon came in. There was an empty seat across from him at the eight-man table. The magician took it.

The level of magic Simon needed to read the cards would be detectable by Orthon. He knew this, counted on it. He wanted the demon to know against whom and what he was playing. On that night the other players did not matter. It would be just the two of them in an open-faced game. By the look in the demon's eyes, he knew this and did not like it. He glared in challenge, Simon smiling in reply.

By the end of the night, most of the money on the table was in front of either Simon or Orthon.

Momma appeared in the doorway. "Closing time," she announced. As the other gamblers gathered their money and personal effects neither Simon nor Orthon moved.

"One more hand, Momma, please," Simon asked. "Then we'll be gone." There was something in his voice.

"One more hand. Should I stay?"

"It would be best if you did not."

Trusting Simon, she left them alone.

"Who are you?" the demon asked. Simon mentioned a name he used decades ago, one he had relinquished when it became too well known in certain lower circles. Orthon nodded in recognition.

"They sent you, didn't they?"

Simon smiled, shook his head. "You know that name. That means you know me well enough that no one 'sends' me, especially not one of Them. Let's just say I was provided with information and decided to act."

Orthon spat on the floor, causing the carpet to sizzle. There would be a burn hole there come morning. "Bastards," he said, then cursed Them in a language unfit for human ears and unpronounceable by most human tongues.

"Imagine that," Simon said in plain English, as if he had not understood most of what Orthon had said, "not being able to trust the Masters of the Pit. I'm shocked."

"What do you want, sorcerer?"

"Magician, if you please. Or mage if you prefer. I haven't sorced in decades. As for what I want, you have in your possession several contracts, promissory notes for debts owed you, payable in cash or the signer's own self."

"And if I do, what business is it of yours?"

"Actually, it's more of a hobby. And it's no concern of mine if some jackass knowingly offers himself or his services to you in exchange for something he thinks will make his miserable life better. But it's different when you trick them into signing."

Orthon shrugged. "I'm a demon. It's what I do. So you want me to just hand over these contracts?"

"Of course not," Simon replied. "As you say, you're a demon. Something for nothing is not what you do."

"Damned straight. So what are you suggesting?"

"Just as I told Momma, one last game."

The demon snorted. "My contracts against what – this?" he gestured toward the money on the table and snorted again. "This means nothing to me. It is merely a means to my ends."

"I've read the Book," Simon said calmly. "I know the Names."

At this Orthon grew silent, then looked worried. Finally, "You're lying."

In the same language with which the demon had cursed the Masters of the Pit, Simon said a name. It was a single word which, if translated into English, would mean "Possessor of Bodies." Immediately Orthon doubled up as if he had a kidney stone and a massive migraine both at the same time.

As Orthon writhed in pain, Simon said, "Now you know I'm not lying. And by the way, I know another name that means "Lord of Slaves."

"How many?" the demon asked as he began to recover. "How many do you know?"

"All of them. How many contracts do you hold?"

"A devil's dozen." Thirteen. "An even exchange then. My contracts for an equal number of Names."

Simon shook his head. "No. It has to be what I suggested. A single game. All of your contracts against an equal number of names. Winner takes all. Oh, and we use that deck." The magician pointed to a deck on another table, one neither of the two had handled that night. "Just to make it interesting."

"What game?" Orthon asked, nodding his assent.

"High card. You cut first. If my card is higher, I win."

Orthon was quick to agree, realizing that the way Simon had phrased the rules had given him a slight advantage and knowing that, if he lost, there were more foolish humans out there waiting to be tricked.

They moved to the other table, sat down. Simon gestured to the demon. "Your cut."

Orthon drew from the middle of the deck. Threw it in the center of the table. Queen of Diamonds. To beat him his opponent would have to draw a king or ace.

Simon reached out, nonchalantly taking the top card from the deck. Without turning it over he laid it atop the Queen.

"You're not going to look at it?" Orthon asked, suddenly suspecting that something had gone amiss.

"I don't have to," Simon said. "Whatever it is, by its very

position, it's higher than your card."

There was no denying that, or the fact that Simon had not specified that his card would be higher in rank, just that it be "higher." And it clearly was.

"You … you tricked me."

"I'm a magician. It's what I do. And now, the contracts, please."

There was no chance that Orthon would renege. Having made the agreement, he was bound by it. Reluctantly he reached into an inner pocket of his jacket and handed over thirteen slips of paper. Simon counted them, then,

"There's one missing."

"Thirteen. It's what we agreed on."

"We agreed on *all* your contracts. That would include the one for the body you're wearing."

Having said this, Simon felt control of Orthon's body pass to him.

Simon let the demon struggle against him for a few minutes then said,

"I could order you to find a church, enter it, and sing hymns of praise to the Creator. But I'll be merciful and so leave you in my debt. Leave this place, walk four blocks south, then go to Hell."

Fighting Simon's compulsion, the demon stood, left the room and soon the restaurant. Four blocks from now, his body would fall lifeless on the sidewalk. Orthon's self would descend to the Pit, there to be greeted in a variety of painful ways by demons both lesser and greater. It would be some time before he could gather the strength to return to this plane.

Pocketing the money he had won, he left the demon's share for Momma to do with as she pleased. He then left for his apartment, where he could contemplate the problem of what to do with the thirteen bodies over which he now had control.

Paid in Full

Hell is not what most people believe. It is not a lake of fire in which souls are immersed as they eternally burn for their mortal sins. Nor is it, as one French novelist suggested, a possibly locked room filled with people you can't stand and where there is nothing to do but talk to them. And it is not a city in which the damned dwell and suffer constant torture at the hands of their tormentors. The last would be redundant, as there are too many cities this side of Creation where that already happens.

Hell is different for each person. For Alan Conrad it was intense cold, cold that burned his skin worse than fire, cold that caused his teeth to chatter so badly that they soon broke off. As his teeth continued to chatter the exposed nerve endings exploded over and over, filling his mouth with the pain of a dozen toothaches.

The cold also ravaged his body, causing him to shake so badly that his bones snapped one by one, their broken ends rubbing against one another with his every movement.

At first, Alan thought he would go mad. Then he hoped he would, so that in his madness he would come to accept his torment and even enjoy it. But that kind of release is denied those sentenced to the Pit, those who by their actions or inactions chose to abandon their Creator and the Mercy They willingly provide.

In Alan's Hell, he remained alert. And it was his conscious mind that tortured him the most. For all he could think of, all he was permitted to think of, were the choices he had made in life that had led him to the frigid, desolate plane that was the whole of his existence until Judgement, and possibly afterwards. Even through his suffering, he saw the paths he had chosen in life and where they had led him. He was permitted brief glimpses of the lives he might have led had he taken other paths. Most of those lives were better than the one he had lived. None were worse.

Time and again his choices played out before him. Time and

again he was shown how it was these choices that had condemned him. And all Alan Conrad could do was watch and suffer.

For this was Hell, and Hell was punishment eternal.

Or so he believed.

It was a millennium after he had first been damned, or maybe it was the same day he had been cast into the Pit – time has no meaning in Heaven or Hell – that Alan began to consider others in his life. The women he had abused, the friends he had betrayed, the people he had robbed, the men he had killed – all these were affected by his choices, and most had suffered because of them. At first, he took comfort that at least he had made others suffer the way he was suffering. Then he slowly realized that while he was the cause of their suffering, it was their suffering that caused him to be where he was. And so he hated them for being weak, for allowing themselves to be victims. Another day or millennium later, he accepted that he was the cause of their suffering and thus the cause of his own. And so he hated himself for what he had done. Hate led to regret, and regret to sorrow, and sorrow to enlightenment, and enlightenment to repentance.

But Alan Conrad was still in Hell. And he knew there would be no escape until Judgement, which might be a day or a millennium away.

Alan's acceptance that his punishment was right and just did not lessen the pain of the cold or his memories. But perhaps it did allow him to remember something of his final days alive. It was a week before someone he had sold to the cops for a walk was released on bail and paid him for his betrayal with two shots to the head. There was a card game, one at which he lost his money and left his marker. It was the memory of this game and this marker that ignited a small spark of hope in his tortured soul. And before the warmth of this hope could be extinguished by the ice of Hell, Alan Conrad sent a desperate plea to whatever or whoever might be able to hear him.

"Help me!"

"I'm not paying."

This was not the first time Simon Tombs had gotten this response when trying to collect on the promissory notes he had won from the demon Orthon. There had been thirteen notes in all, gambling debts. Simon had won them in a poker game at Fortuna's, a restaurant and not-so-secret card parlor just off of Broadway in Baltimore's Fells Point.

One of the debtors had died, leaving twelve. Seven of these had already left their money with Momma Fortuna. She, in turn, had passed the money on to Simon, who donated it to various worthy causes.

Simon would just as soon had let the gamblers keep their money. Orthon had, after all, won it in a less than honest manner. But in this case, that was not an option.

As he tried to explain the woman sitting in front of him. As he had explained to the others before her.

"Ms. Dunn, this is not an ordinary IOU. Please read what it says."

Taking a copy of the note from Simon, Amy Dunn read it aloud. "I pledge myself to pay the sum of two thousand, five hundred dollars to the bearer of the note within ninty days. So what? Gambling debts are not legal and you weren't the one I borrowed it from in the first place."

Simon had the patience of a … that is, he had the patience of a man who had lived a long time and had dealt with many different kinds of people. Most human, some not. This past week had tried even his equanimity as he tracked down and collected on the debts before they came due.

"Please take a closer look at what you signed, Ms. Dunn. There is a slight space between the 'y' and the 's' of myself. It means that you did not pledge yourself but rather *your self*, your very being. If your debt is not paid by the end of this week then, and there's no easy way to put this, you belong to me, to do with what I will. I'll have complete control over your body and your actions."

Amy, of course, did not believe him and she told him so in the coarsest of terms. So like the three people before her, he had no choice but to convince her.

"You're a sick, perverted bastard," Amy said, getting up from her kitchen chair and heading for her phone. "I'm calling the cops and have your ass thrown in jail. A pretty boy like you won't last long there."

She was wrong about that. Simon had been in jail, several times in fact. He had done very well in all of them, escaping from most and taking over the rest.

"Your phone won't work," he said calmly. When Amy failed to get a dial tone, she reached for her cell. "That won't work either. In fact, Ms. Dunn, none of your electronics will work, except for the TV in your living room, and that will only play CNN, a home shopping channel, and reruns of Green Acres."

Just then the voice of Eddie Albert could be heard from the living room singing "Farm living is the life for me." As the annoying theme song played on and on Simon said,

"And in case you're not yet convinced, try moving."

Amy could not.

"Your signature on that note was a part of you," Simon explained. "That and your stated refusal to pay your debt has already given me some power over you. Not enough to make you do what I want, but just enough so that I can keep you from doing what you want.

"You see, Ms. Dunn," he told the thankfully stricken speechless woman, "the creature from whom you borrowed the money was a demon from Hell. He would have used your body and the bodies of the others to prolong his presence on Earth. It is my nature that I could not allow that. So I went all in and won the debts from him. But they still have to be paid. Or else control over your very self falls to me. This is a taste of what that would be like. I don't want that kind of power, and I'm sure you don't want me to have it. Now, will you please pay up? You may speak."

As Amy tried to move and failed, all she could do was think of a cowardly lion who kept repeating "I do believe in spooks. I do! I do!" Amy had not believed in much in her life but now she at least believed in Simon Tombs.

As had Simon had expected, she said, "I'll pay." The others had agreed to pay as well.

Once Simon allowed Amy to move, she sat right down. Once she was seated, her demeanor changed. In a somewhat seductive voice she asked,

"I said I'll pay and I will. But does it have to be in money?" She looked upwards toward what Simon presumed to be her bedroom. "I've always been attracted to strong men and my husband won't be home for a few hours yet. Maybe we can work something out by you working something in?"

It was not the first time that week Simon had received that offer. Another woman and one of the men had made similar propositions. Simon had quickly but politely turned down the man. The woman had been very attractive and under other circumstances … but he believed that encounters of that sort should be between equally willing partners with no hint of coercion to spoil the fun or taint one's soul. As both the man and woman were truly short on funds he had them agree to do volunteer work – her at an animal shelter and him at a soup kitchen – and returned their notes.

"As tempting as your offer is, as tempting as you are, Ms. Dunn," Simon said gallantly, "I'm afraid I must decline. Another time, perhaps. Now, will you be paying with cash or by check?"

She wrote him a check. On handing it to him, she said, "Too bad. I think we're both missing out on a swell time."

"My loss, Ms. Dunn. As I said, perhaps another time."

As he left the Dunn residence Simon reminded himself to mail Amy her note as soon as her check cleared.

Just one to go, he thought, not knowing just how wrong he was.

Usually, when he was in his own apartment, Simon Tombs slept very soundly. He had warded it against supernatural and demonic incursions. These protections also worked against mundane threats as well. The last thief who tried to break in having been found in the street below with second-degree burns on his hands and no idea how they got there. A certain homicide detective, having heard of the incident and knowing where Simon lived, had her suspicions. But fortunately for Simon suspicions aren't proof.

So it was strange that Simon woke up at the time when the

night had begun to give way to the day, the time when all forces were equally strong and angels might meet demons on neutral ground.

At first, he thought it a rare headache. But then what he took to be throbbing in his head developed into a small, pleading voice crying "Help me!" over and over again.

He knew it for a sending of some kind. But before he could get into the right frame of mind to trace the voice back to its origin it faded. Try as he might, he could not retrieve it.

If it's important they'll call back, he thought, then turned over and went back to sleep, dreaming of David Hedison, Patricia Owens, and flies with human faces.

The Fayette Street garage to which Simon had traced Ferguson Parks, the last debtor whose paper he held, had seen better days. The sign declaring it to be "Parks Garage and Repair" was faded and pockmarked with what he believed to be bullet holes. The customer door, being closed and padlocked, discouraged any walk-in business. But the garage door was slightly ajar and so Simon opened it and slipped in.

The interior was dark and lacked the oil and gasoline smell he'd come to associate with such establishments. There was also a distinct lack of any sounds indicating repairs taking place. As Simon's eyes adjusted he saw why.

There was only one car in the place. It had three tires, a smashed windshield, and a layer of dust that suggested that it had been there for at least one presidential term. There were also two large, nasty looking men who had interrupted their card game to stare at him.

"What the hell do you want?" asked the larger of the two.

"I'm here to see Mr. Parks on a matter of business. Would either of you … gentlemen be him?"

"You a cop?" asked the nastier looking one.

"No," Simon said quickly and in a tone of voice that suggested he had just been insulted. "A private citizen with, as I said, business with Mr. Parks. If neither of you is him, please fetch him for me like good little boys."

It was a deliberate provocation, one with which Nasty took

exception. He quickly came at Simon, only to smash into the garage door which Simon had closed on entry. When Nasty tried to get up, Simon kicked him so he would stay down.

By this time the large one was on his feet. Simon stopped his advance by placing his hand inside his suit coat in a well-understood gesture. The large one sat back down but not before making his own well-understood gesture toward Simon.

"And the same to you," Simon replied. "Now would you please tell Mr. Parks that a fellow player from Fortuna's would like a word?"

The large man took out a flip phone. Using it in intercom mode he said, "Boss, some guy to see you. Said it's about a poker game." Interpreting the static he said to Simon, "He'll be right down."

By then Simon had figured out what was going on. Extending his senses he was able to detect the faint hum of hidden electronic devices, which explained the static on the flip phone as well as the unmarked white van he had passed coming in. Suddenly a not so ordinary errand had become an opportunity for adventure and fun.

A small, stocky man appeared in the back, having come down the stairs from the second floor. *No doubt where the real business is conducted*, Simon thought. *I wonder if he knows, or cares, who is listening in.*

"I know you," Parks said on seeing Simon. "Draw poker, sometimes stud. Conservative. You usually win but not much. What do you want?"

Simon recognized Parks as one of Madame Fortuna's regulars. *Maybe, just maybe this will be easy*, he hoped.

"You're a Texas Hold'em player. Pretty good as I recall, except against this fellow." Simon handed Parks a copy of the IOU he had signed.

"You ain't that fellow, Mr. …?"

"Tombs. Simon Tombs." That should give the guys in the van something to think about. "And I won this paper from him. I'm here to collect."

Parks shook his head then tore up the paper. "Sorry you wasted a trip, Mr. Tombs. But as I said, you ain't that fellow. And I don't think his game was quite on the level. So you'll have to look elsewhere for your money."

Simon could have given Parks the same treatment he had given the other reluctant debtors. He could have frozen Parks's muscle and maybe compelled the man to go upstairs and get his money. But Simon decided that it might be more fun to do things a little differently.

"I understand, Mr. Parks. But my understanding does not cancel the debt. You know where to leave the money. Or else I'll be back to collect in five days."

"You'll waste another trip, Mr. Tombs, and you might get your suit messed up."

Simon gave Parks a smile, the kind of a smile that had he known Simon better would have prompted Parks to pay up right away, with an added bonus for his time and trouble. Then he said, "If that's the case you should have more and better men on hand. I'll be sure to wear an old suit."

With that, he smiled again and left.

Simon had not walked a half block before two men in suits much less expensive than his stopped him. "FBI," one said, showing credentials. "Would you mind coming with us, Mr. Tombs?"

"Do I have a choice?"

"Not really, sir."

"Then lead on."

Simon was driven to the Regional FBI office in Woodlawn, just southwest of Baltimore. There he was left in a windowless room that contained three chairs, a table and, for the moment, him. *No one-way mirror*, he observed, *that could only mean …*

It was their own fault, Simon later decided, leaving him alone in a room with nothing to do. Standard interrogation technique to soften one up. It worked on most people. Simon Tombs, however, was not that kind of person. There were those who would argue that he had long ago stopped being any kind of person.

As in the garage, there was the hum of electronics. This being an FBI building, to his senses the hum was loud and pervasive, coming from all directions. With nothing else to do, he concentrated on the noises closest to him. All four upper corners. The room was covered for sight and, no doubt, sound. For now.

The door opened and two agents walked in. A man and a woman. The woman sat down in front of him. The man stood by the door, as if Simon might do something foolish like trying to leave of his own accord.

"I'm Special Agent Buckley, Mr. Tombs. Behind me is Special Agent Tanner. We have some questions for you."

"Always happy to cooperate with the authorities," Simon said with a smile that seemed genuine.

"That's not what we've been told," Tanner growled from his position at the door.

"You've been talking to Detective Hood, haven't you? In fact, unless I miss my guess, she's somewhere out there listening in."

Simon looked up at the ceiling. "Katie, if you're out there come join the party."

There was a pause, then a knock on the door. Detective Caitlin Hood of the Baltimore Police Homicide Unit walked into the room.

"Have a seat, Katie. We seem to have an empty chair."

"I've told you not to call me that," Hood said as she sat beside Buckley.

"No," Simon replied, "You told me not to call you 'Caitlin.' Now, which don't you want to be called? I'd call you 'Robin' but that's mixing too many stories together."

"Let's get back to the matter at hand," Buckley said with no little irritation. "How do you know Ferguson Parks?"

"I don't. I only just met him today."

"Why did you go see him?"

"You should know, Agent Buckley. You or your agents were listening in. He owes me money, a gambling debt. I went there to collect."

"Gambling is illegal, Mr. Tombs."

"Go down to Russell Street and tell that to all those people at the Horseshoe Casino. Now, what is it you really want to know?"

"As I said, the extent of your involvement with Parks. He's a gun runner, a narcotics dealer, and a human trafficker. We're looking at him for enterprise corruption. He's also a suspect in three Baltimore City homicides. Now what can you tell us about him?"

Simon shrugged. "He's a lousy poker player. He always waits for the flop before deciding to fold. Other than that, not a thing. But I hope to see him again in a few days. If anything comes up I'll be sure to talk really loud."

Before either agent could replay to that, Simon turned toward Hood.

"I just remembered, Katie, your birthday was last week and I didn't even get you a card. Since you always decline my dinner invitations I'll have to get you something nice to make up my lapse. Maybe after my business with Parks is over."

Another growl from Tanner. "Your business with Parks is over, Mr. Tombs."

"Five thousand dollars," Simon said quietly.

"What?"

"Five thousand dollars, Agent Buckley. That's how much Parks owes me. Pay his debt and I'll have no more business with him. In fact, I'll give you the special agent discount – three thousand dollars and I'll even declare it on my taxes. No? Well, then, as much fun as this hasn't been I think I'll leave now. Unless we have other business?"

Buckley looked at Hood. The detective shook her head. "Tombs is a lot of things but he's never lied to me. If he says he's not involved with Parks then he's not."

"You're free to go, Mr. Tombs."

Simon stood. "Do I get a ride home?"

In what was obviously a much-practiced gesture, Tanner handed Simon $2.75 in change. "Bus fare. Have a nice trip home."

It was a petty gesture but one well played. Simon smiled and nodded. He jingled the change in his hand. "I'll be sure to declare this as well. Katie, Julian, Diane, it's been fun."

It was five minutes after a uniform guard escorted had him out of the building that Agents Tanner and Buckley realized that they had not told Simon their first names. "You get used to it," was all the explanation Detective Hood offered. Later, when they tried to replay the recording of the interview they found it nothing but static.

It was a long bus ride from Woodlawn back to his apartment. On the way, Simon thought about his meeting with Ferguson Parks. If the man was as black as the FBI painted him, his debt was greater than the money he owed Simon. *If* Tanner had been telling the truth. He had been told bigger lies by better liars and he was sure the agent was telling what she believed was the truth.

Still, it wouldn't hurt to check, he decided. He then turned his attention to the plea for help he had received. He would deal with later that night, he told himself.

Once back in his apartment Simon made some calls – to police detectives who owed him favors, to federal officials who sometimes relied on his talents and abilities, to less savory characters who would for the right incentive – money, threats, fear – reveal dark secrets about darker people.

An hour later Simon was convinced that Ferguson Parks was a very bad man. Simon knew how to deal with bad men and those who aided and abetted them. He revised his plans for his next meeting with Parks. Detective Hood was not going to like her present. Still, it was the thought that counted.

The voice did not wake him that night. Instead, it intruded into his dreams. He was with an actress he had known some time ago and they were just about to renew their intimate acquaintance when …

"Help me!"

Before going to bed, Simon had prepared. His dreaming mind began to trace the sending even as his conscious one strove to catch up. When they united, he found himself on a desolate, frozen plane. The cold bit into him, his body shivering as his teeth chattered violently.

He was alone. He should not have been. The one who sent the plea should have been there. That's the way the dream plane worked.

So this is not the dream plane. Simon verified this by trying to create a warming fire. He failed.

The cold got worse. There was tingling in his extremities and he knew that soon he would be losing feeling in his fingers and toes.

Time to wake up. Again, he failed.

Not good. Where in the hell have I gotten myself into?

"Help me!"

This time the voice came from inside him, as if echoing his thoughts. But he hadn't thought it. So he was not alone. And this shivering suffering body was not his. Or so he hoped.

Shutting off his awareness of the body in which he found himself brought him some relief. "Who are you?" he mentally asked. "Where are you?" he added.

His only answer was a sense of connection to whomever it was followed by another "Help me," before he was pulled from the body so violently that he awoke with a start.

Pins and needles in his toes and fingers as warmth rushed back into them.

That was unpleasant. Just what in hell was that all about?

Then with a chill that was nothing like that from the frozen plane, he got the suspicion he had just answered his own question.

"So who do I know in Hell?" he asked himself over a late night, early morning cup of Zeke's Coffee. The answer was far too many souls, some of which he had personally sent there. But none of them would have the kind of connection that could draw him to them. Nor was it the kind of trap a creature of the Pit would set. This was personal. Simon had felt the bond before it was severed. And it would have to be a strong bond to reach all the way from Perdition.

Another cup of coffee and two Berger cookies later Simon put it together. The notes. Outside of Parks's, there was still one outstanding debt. One that was now overdue, giving Simon control over that person's self, that person's soul.

More research. Like Ferguson Parks, Alan Conrad had not been a very nice man. In fact, had Conrad still been alive, Simon might have pointed him toward Parks then dealt with the survivor.

I have to start playing cards with a better class of gamblers, he thought when his contacts and his Internet browsing revealed that

Conrad had probably done enough in his life to warrant punishment in the next.

Simon understood why Conrad had sent his plea to him. What bothered him was why. Why had he been permitted to reach out? Why was he given this tenuous thread of hope? Simon could think of only one reason. As he watched the sun rise over Baltimore, he knew what he had to do.

He was on his way to his study, which is where he practiced his more serious magic, when he saw the woman standing in his living room.

She was plain, her hair a non-descript brown. Her figure was covered by a bulky sweater, which may have served to conceal a weight problem. Her jeans were faded and somewhat worn at the knee. Her feet were in sandals and did not quite touch the floor.

Looking past her outward appearance, Simon saw a radiant beauty not of this world, an aura reflecting the Divine on whose behalf this being had come.

Resisting the urge to genuflect – one does not worship the messenger, however holy the message – Simon simply bowed. The being smiled, returned his bow, and called him by a name he had not heard for several decades. It was his birth name, and he had thought it lost and forgotten. But apparently not to the Ones who know the hairs on your head and the sparrows in the sky.

"I go by Simon these days," he dared to say.

The reply came in a whisper, yet he clearly heard every word.

"Well then, 'Simon,' know that the path you are taking is a perilous one. One not to travel lightly, one that has not been attempted in several hundred years."

Simon sighed. "And yet I must, unless it is forbidden."

Another smile, one Simon did not doubt would have lit up a darkened room. "It would not be the first forbidden path you have trod."

"I do not seek Paradise this time, but rather a single soul."

"A soul condemned to the Pit."

"A soul pledged to me and so under my care. A soul who has truly repented."

"You know this?"

"Why else would he be allowed hope where it is to be abandoned?"

"The words of a poet."

"But none the less true. Am I right?"

The angel nodded. "There will be a Choice – a hope of redemption, the risk of oblivion. And consequences either way. The choice will be his, the consequences yours. Do you accept this?"

Simon pictured himself trapped for all eternity, freezing in a wasteland, having freed Conrad only to take his place, his cries of "Help me" going unheeded. Just a moment of doubt, then he put his trust in the Mercy and Justice of the Ones who had sent Their messenger.

"I do. I must."

"Very well. Take care, Simon. For a great responsibility will be yours."

The angel was gone. Simon had not turned away. He had not blinked. Yet she was gone. Despite the daylight shining through the windows, the room seemed darker.

"I had hoped to catch a ride," he said aloud. "This time I didn't even get bus fare."

Simon went to his study. Sitting down, he took from his desk drawer the note that gave him the self of Alan Conrad. He stared at it, thinking of the frozen plane, establishing a connection. He felt a tug on his soul. He imagined a cord tying them together. The cord became a rope, and the rope a bridge. He was on the bridge, looking down at a river where a hooded ferryman was conveying souls to Judgement.

He walked the bridge forever, or maybe just a moment. It ended on a plane of ice and snow where the cold bit into one's skin and the wind howled and cut like a blade. But he was not cold. This was not his punishment.

The rope was still in his hand. Simon thought to turn to see if the bridge still stood but he thought of Orpheus and Lot's wife and did not dare. He pulled the rope and the air filled with souls, all of them pleading "Take me, save me, help me. I repent, I'm sorry. Help me!"

These he ignored.

There were others. They were few and did not cry out, but hovered around him in silent hope. "I've sinned," they seemed to say. "And I truly repent those sins, for Their sake and not mine. Save who you will. I accept my fate."

I cannot save them all, not even the few who deserve it. Simon thought as the full weight of the responsibly the angel spoke of settled on him. *I will always have this rope, and the bridge will always be there.*

"I seek Alan Conrad," he cried out loud. All the souls but one faded away. This one was shivering, and his feet and hands were black with frostbite.

"I am, or rather was, Alan Conrad," he somehow managed to say.

"You still are. My name is Simon Tombs, and you owe me money."

The absurdity of this statement, his contact with someone, anyone after who knew how long, told Conrad that somehow his prayer had been answered. He dared to say, "I'm afraid I left my wallet in my other pants."

Simon smiled. A joke in Hell. Somewhere far below, those who collectively were known as Satan were wailing and gnashing their teeth at the added pain.

"Alan Conrad," Simon solemnly, "I offer you a choice. Return to your place of punishment and suffer until the Final Judgement, or be released, not knowing if that release leads to reward or oblivion."

"Release," Conrad said quickly, as if Simon might change his mind and withdrawal his offer. "If reward I will be humbled and grateful. If I cease to be it is less than I deserve. I do not want to go back. I do not want to despair and curse the Names and be lost forever."

Like the angel had earlier, the soul of Conrad was there and then he was not. Unlike earlier, Simon felt something enter him. It was not Conrad's soul but he had received something from the man.

The rope faded. As did the bridge. And then so did he, only to wake with a start at his desk.

It could have been a dream but for the power Simon now felt inside him, power he could use any way he chose, for good or for ill. Whether it was power from a redeemed soul or from one that no longer existed he didn't know. *Every trip across that bridge, every tug on that rope,* he realized, *will bring more power.* The idea scared and humbled him, and he prayed that he would bear the responsibility wisely.

With this thought in his mind, Simon looked down at his desk. Then he started laughing. Where before the desktop had been empty, there was now $2.75 in change. Leaving his study, he went out on to his balcony. Looking up at the sky he said out loud. "Well played, Sirs, well played."

Simon's job, however, was not over. There was still one more debt to collect. He did not wish to be tied to Ferguson Parks when that ungodly soul met his fate.

Simon took the bus to Parks's garage. Why not, he had the fare. As he had promised, he wore an old suit. And as he had suggested, Parks had brought in more men.

There were five of them this time. There were Nasty and his large partner. None of the other three would win any beauty contests and were long shots for Miss Congeniality.

Unnecessarily Simon said, "I'm here to see Parks."

He had expected a remark along the lines of "Well, he doesn't want to see you." Instead, without a word, they started coming for him.

He could have messed with their brains; shutting them down, killing them, putting them into comas, or giving them seizures that would cause them to convulse and soil themselves. But he didn't think that would be an appropriate use of his newly given power. Instead, he slowed them down and made them clumsy, then he took his time with them.

He punched, he kicked, he broke some bones and shattered others. Nothing lethal, nothing that could not be treated, but the five would be left with painful reminders of the encounter for quite some time. He hoped whatever prison they were sent to had a good hospital ward.

When it was over, when he was alone on the floor with five unconscious men, Simon did not have to call out for Parks. He did not have to search for him. Parks's note was past due. All Simon had to do was exert his will.

Parks fought him. As he came down the stairs from the second floor Parks fought him, struggling to go back up even as he descended. Simon found a chair, sat down, and waited patiently until Parks was standing in front of him.

While he let Parks get a good look at his fallen men, Simon mentally reached out and disabled the hidden electronic devices. What he had to say to Parks was not for the ears of those in a white van.

"You should have paid me the money, Fergie. You really should have. Then I would have been out of your life, these men would not be in need of medical treatment, and you would not be under my control. But you had to welch, had to play the tough guy. And so here we are, and here's what you're going to do.

"In a minute or two, I've going to leave you, but not before turning on the microphones that have been recording you for the past several weeks. You will then tell the truth about the three murders of which you are suspected. When the feds rush in, which they no doubt will, you will cooperate fully. You will waive your rights, you will answer all their questions, you will not seek any deals or special consideration. Nod if you understand me."

Clearly wanting to call Simon every filthy name he could think of, Parks instead nodded his head.

"Good, and when you're answering their questions, when you're testifying in court, when you're sitting in your prison cell waiting for the inevitable retribution from those against whom you have testified, remember this. All you had to do was pay me the money. Oh, and there's one more thing."

Simon told him what that was. Then he stood. Again reaching out with his mind, he restored the electronic devices to functionality.

This time he was not stopped on his way out. He waved to the agents in the van but he doubted they heard him, not with what Parks was saying.

Lacking bus fare, he walked a block to Pulaski Highway and took a cab back home.

An email from Agent Diane Buckley. Attached was an audio file she said Detective Caitlin Hood had to hear. A recording made as the Feds were breaking in on Parks as he started to confess. Hood opened it.

At first, it was a recitation of how he had committed the three murders. Then, the smashing of doors as the agents broke in. Then Parks stopped talking and started singing,

"Happy birthday to you. Happy birthday, Caitlin. Happy birthday from Simon. Happy birthday to you."

Night fell, as it inevitably will. Simon watching a TV show about a fairy who had pink wings and fought crime when his lights dimmed and the shadows grew large in his living room. The shadows then developed teeth and eyes.

It's about time, he thought. He had been expecting this visit. Hitting the record button on the remote, he stood and faced them.

They were sendings from the deepest pit of Hell. He did not think they were there to repent and ask forgiveness for their sins. When they spoke it was with the voice of many, all saying the same thing.

They called him by the name the angel had used, thinking his birth name was his true name.

He laughed in the faces of Hell's worst. "Nice try. Now shall I try some names? I've read the Book, I know some good ones."

The shadows shrank a little. None wanted him to speak their true names, that would give the others power over the one named. And his use of their names would only add to their already unbearable suffering.

"Say what you must then leave me."

"You owe us a soul."

"I owe you nothing. But if I find an unworthy one I'm always willing to send it your way. Is that all?"

"Do not cross the bridge," said the collective voices. "Do not pull on the rope. Ropes break, bridges collapse."

"Thank you for the warning. Now let me leave you with one. Do not trouble me again."

Simon closed his eyes and called on the power he had received from the soul of Alan Conrad. He then shone as bright as had the essence of the angel who had visited him. When he opened his eyes, the Pit creatures were gone, and some of his furniture was slightly singed.

"If they thought those threats would discourage me," he said to no one in particular, "then they don't know me very well."

Or perhaps, he thought, *they know me all too well, and they have planned for my next visit. I suppose I have plans of my own to make.*

Rapunzel's Song

There were times that Simon Tombs was convinced that he was in a story. In some of these tales he was the lead character, but always the hero. In others he was the friend, the passerby, the man who whose actions or words set everything into motion. And in still others he was merely an observer, watching what was going on along with the readers.

The key to this, Simon had long ago decided, was to go with the feeling. To decide what kind of story you were in and what your role was.

This was one of those times.

It started when once again Heather Paul walked through the front door of Sebastian's. Simon was sitting in the same seat as the first time, sipping the same drink, or rather, one just like it. This Heather Paul was very different than the one he had first met two years ago. That Heather had been brutally beaten and violated and had stumbled into Sebastian's in search of help and comfort.

Much to the dismay of the police, Simon had provided both. It was his nature to do so. And it was in his nature to use the powers with which he had been gifted to exact a fitting and permanent vengeance on Heather's assailant, thus upsetting a certain homicide detective who strongly suspected but could not prove his involvement.

Simon had also provided Heather with the means of forgetting her ordeal. He gave her a vial of Lethe water, which would have eased the memory of her assault, erased that memory, or erased her very self, depending on how many drops she used. It was, he believed, both a test and a choice.

This Heather, the one who was approaching his table, was different. She moved with the practiced confidence of one who had suffered greatly but had managed to overcome her pain and even grow stronger from it.

"Simon," she said smiling as she accepted his invitation to sit across from him. "It's been too long," she added by way of a loose apology.

It had been almost twenty months. At first, he had kept in touch with her, and she with him. There was no hint of romance but there was the possibility of friendship. But she, like many of this friends, gradually slipped away from him. Simon was used to this, the inevitable consequences of a very long life.

Heather distancing herself from him Simon put down to the circumstances of their meeting. Despite his helping her, he was still a reminder of the very worst day of her life. A day only the forgetfulness of Lethe could erase.

Speaking of which, suddenly there was the bottle with the waters from that sacred river on the table between them.

"I never opened it," she told him. "But having it gave me the strength and courage to heal. Thank you for it but I don't need it anymore."

"It is real, you know."

"I know." And she did. She had felt his power, knew him for what he was, or thought she did. He was, in reality, much more.

"It is good to see you again, Heather," Simon said. Then, as gently as he could, he asked,

"How can I help you?"

She had the grace to blush and look embarrassed. "I feel awful, Simon, after all you did and the way we lost … I stopped …"

"I understand," he said in a way that gave her both absolution and permission to continue. He had come to her aid when they were strangers. He would not, could not turn her away now.

"His name is Alex Baker. I met him about three months after … the incident. I entered therapy, a group of survivors of traumatic events helping each other. Alex was part of the group."

"And from what did he suffer?"

She hesitated, then "We're not supposed to talk outside the group, but it's important for you to know. Alex was in a cult, and was made to do terrible things."

Simon doubted if at first this Alex was "made" to do anything. In his experience, most people usually did exactly what they wanted.

At least until the thrill of the forbidden wore off and they had most likely dammed themselves. But from the way she talked Heather cared deeply for him so Simon stayed silent. But if Alex was hurting her may God have mercy on him because Simon would not.

"What sort of cult?"

"Something called The Followers of the Greater Key."

Simon had met some of the Greater Key before. He'd walked away from the meeting somewhat damaged. They did not walk away at all.

Heather must have seen something of what Simon was thinking on his face.

"What is it," she asked. "Who are these people? Alex wouldn't say."

"A particularly nasty group. They call up demons and force them to grant them knowledge, answer questions, and do their bidding."

And if your friend Alex was involved with them he will be a long time paying for his sins. Simon thought. Such magic as calling up demons did not come cheap, the price was paid in blood, pain, and lives.

Simon gave Heather an address. "My apartment," he said. "What we have to talk about is best discussed in a safe place."

"Your building has good security?" she asked.

"The building's is so-so. My apartment on the other hand …"

By the time Alex and Heather arrived at seven, Simon had checked and rechecked his "security." He refreshed his spells. All his wards and mystical barriers were firm, and there were several demon traps in place should something slip through. This "something" included Alex. In his long life, Simon had made many enemies, not all of them human. He would not put it past them to use Heather as an unsuspecting judas to get inside his defenses.

Nothing against which Simon had prepared happened. Alex and Heather arrived a little after seven. After introductions and pleasantries, and once everyone had their beverage of choice, Simon asked,

"Alex, how high did you rise with the Greater Key? Magister?

Initiate? Acolyte? Did you use the knife or just hold it and pass it on?"

Heather gave Simon a look that many women had given him many times before, and not all for the same reason. Whatever she would have said or done next was forestalled by Alex's hand touching hers.

"It's okay. If he's going to help he has to know." To Simon he said, "I achieved third rank, if you know what that means."

Simon did. Alex had been part of the congregation and not the priesthood. Third rank meant that he had been called on to perform animal sacrifice and engage in sexual acts with willing and sometimes unwilling partners. He would not have been involved in summonings but his actions had provided the power for the priests to do so.

"Heather, would you please excuse yourself for a moment. Guy talk."

She gave Simon an odd look then turned to Alex. At his nod she decided it was time to freshen up.

"Don't mind the snake," Simon told her. "She likes the cold tile and occasional humidity of the bathroom."

When they were alone, he asked Alex, "What is the nature of your relationship with Heather?"

Slightly put off, Alex responded, "You're not her father."

"No, I'm not," Simon said with just a touch of menace in his voice. "I'm something more. I'm her protector. Now answer the question."

Alex sighed. Since joining the cult he had become very guarded about his personal life. After he left it he became more so. He knew Heather was the same way. But if he was to get help for Frieda...

"Heather and I love each other, and are in love with each other. We are working towards intimacy but – the things I did, what happened to her – we have a ways to go before we can physically express our feelings toward each other. I think I have further to go than she does."

The look Alex gave Simon asked, "Was that enough?" Simon's nod told him that it was. But the magician felt compelled to give a warning,

"If you hurt I will come for you."

"If I hurt her I hope you do."

That decided Simon. Heather was in good hands. This was a man worth helping.

A small cry came from the bathroom. "It seems Heather and Kitty have found each other. She, that is, Heather, should be out soon. Then we can discuss your problem and see about fixing up a happy ending."

It was just then that a familiar feeling came over Simon. He smiled to himself as he looked forward to finding out just what story he was in this time.

Heather rejoined them. "I thought you were joking about the snake."

"Said Adam to Eve once upon a time. Now then, Alex, what is the problem and how can I help?"

"It was my wife Felicia who got us involved with the cult. I didn't realize it until about a year after we'd married but Felicia was one of those people who could never be satisfied. She always wanted more – more money, a nicer house, a better vacation than last year's. Maybe it was her childhood, maybe there was just something wrong inside her, but whatever she had, whatever she did, it wasn't enough.

"Then one day she learned about the Greater Key and how it could make all her wants and desires come true. She got involved, got us involved. And I admit, I went in willingly. By this time I was wrapped up in the whole 'nothing's better than more' thing myself. And when I heard about the rituals ..."

"You mean the sexual rites, the orgies." Simon was starting to like the man but was not about to let him off easy.

"Yes," Alex admitted. "At first I thought the whole cult thing was just a front for the sex. By the time I realized how wrong I was I was in too deep. And Felicia was in deeper. Each chance she got she moved closer toward the inner circle. She moved away from me."

"And eventually you got smart and got out, and now the Key is after you?" Simon supposed.

"I only wish it that simple, Mr. Tombs." Alex took a breath.

"Sometime after we joined we learned that Felicia was pregnant. We assumed the child was mine but … who knows. I've always thought of her as mine." The man's eyes began to tear up. Simon began to suspect the worst.

"Felicia wanted power. The Mistress of the Key wanted our child. My wife made a trade, one for the other. I wish I could say I objected. But I was caught up in my own life and thought only of how much an infant would interfere with it so I just let it happen."

Things were narrowing down for Simon. "What happened to the child?" he asked.

"Frieda," Alex said. "Felicia named her Frieda. To my shame, I don't know what happened to her."

Alex was by then almost crying. While Simon did not think that tears made a man any less of one, he realized that should his guest break down they would never get to the end of what had become the prologue.

"Why did you leave the cult?"

That brought Alex around. He even smiled a little. "Believe it or not, even sex, drugs, and a license to do what thou wilt pales after a time. First it became boring. Then after many long years asleep I woke up and had to leave."

Heather had been sitting at Alex's side the whole time. He squeezed her hand. "It was only after I left the cult that I began to realize all they had … all we had done. The group where I met Heather saved me. Heather saved me."

"The love of a good woman will do that," Simon said. It was time to get things back on track. "When did you remember Frieda?"

"A few session ago. The nightmares started again shortly after. That's when Heather told me about your …special talents. I need to know what happened to my child. What I may have done to her. Can you help me …" Alex looked at Heather, again squeezed her hand. "Can you help us?"

Simon thought for a moment, then "Maybe."

An evil witch, a first-born exchanged for something greatly desired. Simon knew what tale he had fallen into. And what to look for. He also knew what dangers threatened, what price might have to be paid. He just had to make sure that he was not the one to pay it.

Simon considered the elements of the tale. There may or may not be a garden. There would be a tower, one difficult to enter.

"How old would Frieda be now?"

Alex subtracted dates in his head. "She turns nine next week,"

All numbers have magic to them. Each has a different use. One, three, five and the like are primes, containing themselves and nothing else. Multiply five or six by itself and the answer will always end with five or six. Continuation. Nine was the symbol for renewal. Multiply any number by nine then add the answer down to one digit. It will always be nine. A summoning for a rebirth, immortality maybe. Frieda did not have much time.

"Where were your meetings held? No, never mind. It's the girl I need and not the group." Simon thought for a moment. *How did the prince…?*

Music and hair. The first had led him to the princess. The second had granted him entry.

"It won't be easy," he told the couple. "No, forget I said that. It will be close to impossible. There is difficulty and danger, much danger, ahead. There may not be a happy ending for any of us. At best, there will be a steep price."

"Whatever it is, I'll pay it."

"We'll pay it," Heather said and Simon wished she hadn't.

"Fate takes offers like yours seriously. Are you sure? We may already be too late. The Greater Key may have already used the girl. Infants make powerful sacrifices. The best we can hope for is vengeance. And you have enough to atone for already, Alex."

There was pain and resolve in Alex's answer. "I have to know. And once I do, I can … we can decide what to do."

"Very well. Leave me your number then leave me alone. I'll call you when it's time. Right now I have to plot against the ungodly."

The wife first. Simon needed her. Needed her to compose the song. Fortunately for him these days it was hard for anyone to hide.

No magic was needed. A call to Alex gave him Felicia's maiden name, her social security number, her last known address, and her work schedule. There followed a session on the computer. Felicia still had her old job to which she walked from her downtown condo.

Unlike the ones that imprison maidens, condo towers are ridiculously easy to get into. Even the ones with doormen. Especially the ones with doormen.

This one had a doorwoman, a very good one Simon decided from the way she studied everyone who came in before making sure they were expected and welcome.

The dragon at the gate. A different story but that didn't help Simon. What did was the man who left as he was approaching. After waiting for him to get out of the woman's field of vision, Simon cast a small befuddlement.

"Sorry," he said as she opened the door for what she believed was the tenant who had just left. "Forgot something."

Walking past the tower's guardian he made for the elevators before she could ask him a question he couldn't answer.

Felicia lived in apartment 1105. It had a strong door and good locks. Simon had a special relationship with both.

"This door is all doors. All doors are this door."

He said this once, then twice. On the third time, he inserted the key to his own apartment, which is protected by more than fickle locks that would yield to just anyone who asked.

He was leaving traces of magic for those who knew how to look. Still, he entered. It could not be helped. He had thought about dropping a token or two from a rival cult group just to sow confusion but decided against this. Baltimore did not need another mage war. The last had been hard enough to cover up.

He found what he needed in a hairbrush in the bedroom and in the trashcan in the bathroom. Hair to weave the spell. The spell to find the tower. The tower to rescue the maiden.

No spells on the way out. "Good day, Pamela," he said with a smile.

She spent the rest of the day wondering just who he was and how he knew her name.

That evening, as the day faded into night and the powers of

light and dark were for a time as one, Simon braided the few blonde strands of hair he'd taken from Felicia's apartment into the darker hair he'd gotten from Alex. The charm it gave him was small, but it was enough.

Every person has their own song, a melody unique to them. The rush of blood through the veins, the beat of the heart that drives the blood, the lungs breathing air. There are the firings of neurons and the quantum rhythms of mind and thought. The spark that animates our souls sings of the Divine while the embers from the Fall moan for the Profane. All combine into a single melody that more than fingerprints and more than DNA defines who and what we are.

With the charm from the hair of her parents cupped loosely in two hands, Simon sat in his darkened workroom and listened for Frieda's song. It was easy to hear. Alex's was strong in his mind's ear as was Felicia's. He heard their families' tunes as well, back to the third generation. One by one he filtered them out. Soon there was but one left. It was faint as if far in the distance. But it was there. He could follow it.

And like the prince in the forest he did. Leaving his body behind, his mind followed the song. Out of the city, east toward the bay, over the bridge, and so to the city on the ocean. That was as far as he could go.

"Ocean City?" Heather asked when told Alex her where his daughter was. "Where in Ocean City?"

"I don't know. I went as far as the spell could take me. To go any further I'll have to, well, go further."

"I'm going with you."

"We're going with you, Alex and me. And before either of you brave men object remember, I've been through my own Hell. I survived it once and will again to save Frieda."

Simon smiled. Like her chosen mate, she was someone worth helping. Still,

"I remind you that there will be a price."

"And Alex and I both said that if necessary we would pay it."

"So you did. We are three and three is a good number.

Tomorrow our quest begins in earnest. Until then, *carpe noctem*. Leave nothing unsaid or undone. For it may your last chance."

They left to do whatever it is two people in love might do when faced with their last night together. Simon spent his night anticipating threats both occult and mundane. Then he rested. In the morning he dressed. At the last minute, he put into his pocket the vial containing the waters of Lethe Heather had returned to him. If the price she or Alex had to pay was too great there was always the gift of forgetfulness, or oblivion. Either might be a blessing if all went to Hell, or Hell came to them.

When Simon picked up Alex and Heather they had their bags packed and satisfied smiles on their faces. There was an aura of newly found closeness about them and they could not stop touching each other. They both slept most of the way to Maryland's Eastern Shore. Apparently, they had taken his advice and had seized the night and each other. At least if they did not get their everafter they had had one happy night.

As part of his preparations, Simon had considered all the places in Ocean City where Frieda might be hidden. There had to be a tower. That much he knew. But the coastal resort was nothing but high-rise hotels and condos from the Delaware Line south to the Inlet. His initial plan was to check into an available motel and again listen for her song.

But then he remembered another part of the story. He searched hotels and condos by name, finally finding *Le Chateau d'Or*. It was the most exclusive residence on the Eastern Shore, the cost of each apartment more than double the average price. Would-be buyers had to agree to background checks and financial reviews and to submit to probing interviews about their personal lives. And rental to tourists was not allowed.

There was, of course, a three year wait for would-be buyers to even be considered.

A golden castle. A tower almost impossible to get into. Where else could their Rapunzel be?

"Are you sure this is the place?" Heather asked as they viewed *Le Chateau d'Or* from a parking lot across Coastal Highway.

"Certain enough to bet our lives on it," Simon replied, reminding them again of the stakes.

"How do we get in?" Alex wanted to know. "From what I can see the security's tighter than most military bases. No gets in without a key card and even then they have to show ID."

"There's always more than one door," Simon assured them. "And I have a way with doors, however they're spelled."

There was, of course, a service entrance, used by the staff and delivery people, none of whom were around late at night. A glamour cast by Simon caused the video surveillance to ignore them. Once inside,

"Twelve floors. You two up to it?"

"If it gets my daughter back, Simon, I'd do twice as many."

"Then let us climb the golden stairs."

Five flights, easy. The next four, not so easy. The braided talisman in Simon's pocket was warm. That was a good sign. What was not was that Frieda's song was not getting any stronger. In fact, it was fading more and more the higher they got. Simon began to expect that this story had a few more chapters to go.

They rested on the ninth. "We'll need our strength," Simon explained, "should we run into the ungodly."

Ten, eleven, then, finally twelve. The talisman was no warmer than when they had started to climb. The song it had conjured was quiet.

Still, we must go in, Simon thought. As always, the apartment door yielded to his touch. They entered the living room.

"You could have used the elevator."

A cry of recognition from Alex.

"Magister Reynolds!"

Reynolds was not a large man. Indeed, a few inches less and he would not have been allowed on most theme park rides. Simon surmised that his involvement and advancement with the Greater Key was obviously his compensating for his physical shortcomings, both in height and possibly elsewhere. Given the circumstances, Simon decided to not voice these suspicions.

"Who do we have here?" The Magister's voice was surprisingly deep for one so small. "The heretic and his whore. You should have remained with us. You could have done better."

"Steady," Simon cautioned feeling both Heather and Alex about to spring.

"And you," the cult leader addressed Simon. "You're the knight come to rescue the fair maiden. Well, I'm afraid you are too late, much too late. She is ours and has been since her parents gave her up." A nod toward Alex. "Thank you for that. And tonight she will become much more. Not that any of you three can do anything about that."

Simon felt the binding but had no time to counteract it. Whatever magic he had, whatever spells he had prepared were trapped inside him.

"Oh yes, Mr. Tombs, your traces were felt in the mother's apartment. We have heard of you and know of your meddling in matters that do not concern you. Your banishment of Orthon was quite impressive. He will reward us well when we offer you to him."

"I'm sure he would, were you alive to do so," Simon said, since a reply is somewhat mandatory in these situations. Not wishing to wait for the villain to take the time to explain the entirety of his evil plan, Simon quickly took his 9mm pistol from its holster and shot Magister Reynolds in the head.

"Damned foolish these mages," he said as Alex and Heather looked on in shock. "They never think beyond their magics."

"But Simon, Frieda's not here. With the Magister dead how can we find her?"

Apartment 1201 took up the whole floor. As such it had a 360 view of Ocean City and its surroundings. "Don't worry, Heather. I wouldn't have killed him if I thought we needed him. I've been a fool. Like most people I forgot there is another part to this story."

In the original story, when Gothel learned that the prince had discovered Rapunzel, she banished her ward to the wilderness. What she did to the prince was something Simon did not want to think about.

He walked to a back bedroom, looked out a window facing south and west. "I know where to find her. I only pray that we're in time."

Assateague Island was a national park a short drive from Ocean City. It was the home of wild horses, an unofficial nude beach, and many marshes and coves. It was as close to a wilderness they could come.

"You drive," Simon said, throwing his car keys to Alex and leading his charges out the door and down the stairs.

"What will you be doing?"

"Listening to music."

Sitting in the darkness of the back of the car, Alex and Heather silent by his command, Simon sought for and found Frieda's song. They drove south, into Old Ocean City, past the Inlet and across the Kelly Bridge which proclaimed it was 3073 miles to Sacramento, California. Following his directions, Alex soon had them on the road to Assateague.

The parking lot was dark. No park rangers were present. Three cars and a van were already there.

"The party looks like it will be crowded. I'll get us as close as possible then we can decide on a course of action. If we're too late, and we just might be, then you two run like Hell. It might be chasing you."

"What about you?"

"I'll be right behind you, Heather."

Which was a lie. Simon would most likely be trying to banish any demon raised by the Greater Key. With luck, good luck, it would be one whose true name he already knew. With bad luck, well, he never expected to live forever.

"Stay close," he told them. "Heather, hold on to my belt. Alex, hold on to Heather as best you can. I'm sure after last night you know how to do that."

There were trails of sorts, which Simon followed as best he could as the music grew stronger in his mind.

Soon there was a light ahead and they came to a clearing. Portable lights had been set up, creating a brightly lit circle in which about twenty people had gathered, chanting what to Simon's ears was a monotonous dirge. At the arc furthest from where Simon stood was a table which served as a makeshift altar. It appeared as if the ceremony had just started.

This should have been good news, with Simon working his way in the darkness to the other side, waiting for Alex and Heather to create a diversion. When they did he'd snatch the child and run, trusting to luck and his magic to get everyone home safe.

But that was not to be. Watching from the darkness, Simon saw the child Frieda. Her hair, blonde like her mother's, had been newly shorn. She must have been growing it all her life for it had been twisted into lengths of rope and used to bind the sacrifice to the altar.

"There's Frieda," Alex whispered, perhaps a bit too loudly, but no one seemed to have heard. "And that's Felicia tied to the table."

Indeed it was, Sion thought. *She had given up much and climbed high but now she was food for a demon.* He tried to feel sorry for her but was not worried when he couldn't.

"She looks younger than I imagined," he said quietly.

"Eternal youth, part of her deal."

"Not so eternal soon."

"What Frieda doing?" Heather asked.

With the help of an old woman, the Mistress no doubt, the child was climbing on to the altar. She had a wicked looking knife in her hand. Sitting astride her bound mother, she held the blade at the ready, waiting for the right time.

Powerful magic, a child sacrificing its own mother. Whatever demon they were trying to raise must be coming from a deep circle of the Pit. This Simon could not allow, whatever the cost.

And the cost looked to be Frieda's life. At the urging of the Mistress, the child was preparing to plunge the blade into her mother's heart.

He had little choice, and magic would be to no avail. Any spell he cast would not be in time. There was only one element that could stop what was happening – the lead in his 9mm.

He could shoot the Mistress, this story's Gothel, but that would not keep the knife from cutting into Felicia's flesh, from piercing her heart, from ending her life. It would not keep the Furies from one day ravaging the child's soul for the sin of matricide.

The child then. She was already doomed if not damned. The bullet would be quick and might perhaps save her soul. It would knock her off her mother.

The chanting grew louder. There came a look of anticipated joy in the girl's face. Simon took aim.

"Simon," Alex all but shouted as his eyes traced the expected path of the bullet. "What are you doing?"

"What I must. Sorry, Alex."

Heather too knew what was about to happen. "There must be another way," she pleaded.

Must there? Simon asked himself as Frieda raised the knife high. Yes, there must, for the story did not end with Rapunzel's death. Suddenly he saw what it was. Hoping he could deal with the consequences, Simon slightly altered his aim and pulled the trigger, sending a bullet into Felicia's head.

The expected hell did break loose as the cult members turned toward the sound of the shots. Deprived of their sacrifice, they clearly meant to offer up the gunman in its place. Fortunately, Simon was the only one with a gun, or so he thought.

"Can you use this?" he offered the 9mm to Heather. Instead of taking it, she drew a .380 from her purse. "I bought this after I was raped. Learned how to use it too."

"Good girl. Try not to shoot us. Alex, go for the girl. I'll tackle the witch."

As Heather laid down covering fire, Simon and Alex made their way around the circle, keeping to the edge of the darkness. They almost made it.

A bright light enveloped them as the Mistress cursed them. "Close your eyes," Simon shouted a moment too late. Alex collapsed screaming, his hands clutching his face.

And so the story plays out, the price – the blinding. With no time for regrets or what-ifs, Simon emptied his clip into the Mistress. Like the Magister before her, she had no protection against worldly weapons.

"You bastard."

Simon heard a small voice, then a small form crashed into him. Uttering oaths and curses that would be unseemly coming from an adult's mouth, Frieda slashed and stabbed at Simon.

He easily and quickly disarmed her.

"You killed Mother," she screamed then spat at him as he held her tightly at arm's length so as to avoid being kicked.

Once he had the girl subdued, he looked into her eyes. What he saw there were darkness and evil. The Magister had been right. Simon had been too late, too late by nine years. Nine years of being taught, nine years of being indoctrinated, nine years of being corrupted. It would have been better to have killed her.

Heather's words came back to him. *There must be another way.* And again he realized there was. A desperate way, a difficult way, but it was the only other way.

Holding the girl tightly with one hand, Simon took a small vial from his pocket. Forcing her mouth open he poured the waters of Lethe down her throat.

Now she would forget. She would revert back to infancy and forget. Not the happy ending Heather had hoped for – a blinded fiancé and a nine-year-old baby. But that was the price she had offered to pay.

Heather's gunfire had sent most the cult members scurrying. Those that didn't run were lying dead on the ground. The price they paid.

When Heather approached him Simon quickly explained the situation. Just moments away from shock she asked,

"What do we do?"

"We leave this for the authorities to find and make our way back to Baltimore. On the way, we come up with an explanation of why Alex was struck blind and his daughter brain damaged. Now stay strong and help me with …"

A sob from the girl. Of course. She was a baby now and babies cry. And so the last part of the story.

Taking out his handkerchief, Simon blotted Frieda's tears. Then he ran over to the still moaning Alex, forced the man's hands away from his face and wiped his blinded eyes with the tear-dampened cloth.

Alex quickly calmed. He blinked as his vision slowly returned. "What, what happened?" he asked.

"All part of the story," was the only answer he received.

Simon left it to Heather to explain about Frieda as he sent them back to the car. He stayed behind to make sure they left nothing for the authorities to trace back to them.

He was just about done when from behind he heard,

"Master."

He turned. There, loose from her bindings, was Felicia, or rather, her body. Whatever inhabited it was not and probably never had been human.

Felicia was the sacrifice. I spilled her blood. I called up ... something.

Again the woman spoke. "You are the master. I am your servant. How shall I be called?"

Simon's first thought was how to explain Felicia's apparent presence to Alex and Heather. His second was that he was now in an entirely different story.

Scorpion

It was early in the morning. Simon Tombs sat up, fully awake. Unlike the woman in bed next to him, who was sleeping the sleep of the …

"Certainly not the just," Simon said to no one in particular. A smile came to his face. "More likely the just after."

He reflected on how much his companion enjoyed sleeping. He knew why. It was still new to her.

Simon looked down at his companion. She was a well-figured natural blonde. Legally she was in her mid-thirties, but the body lying next to him was that a young woman just shy of twenty, its former owner having sold part of her soul for lifelong youth.

A poor bargain, Simon reflected, given that Felicia Baker's life of youth and beauty lasted only a few short years. It was Simon who had ended it.

A child about to murder its mother, a sacrifice which would permit a creature from the Deep Pit to escape its bondage and wreak havoc on Earth. Simon had time for only one shot. He could have killed the child, *should* have killed the child, but that wasn't part of the story in which he had found himself. Instead, he killed the mother. A bullet fired into Felicia Baker's head ended the ceremony and gravely disappointed the major demon looking forward to a bloody vacation on the mortal plane.

But for once Simon had not thought things through. Blood was spilled on a sacrificial altar and a sharp-witted Pit dweller was quick to take seize the advantage of the now dead and soulless body.

Only to find itself under the control of the one who had slain the victim.

Simon Tombs.

Simon did not want control of a creature of Hell. No matter that the creature was now unmistakably female and very attractive.

"Go back," he said. "Return to the Pit from whence you came."

A bit stilted but that how one spoke to demons.

To his surprise, the demon did not immediately obey.

"You would have one who has been placed under your care and protection return to endless torment?"

Simon knew that he should have said yes and sent her back to Hell. But he had a strong sense of obligation. He was responsible for this … woman. And having been to Hell, however briefly, he was reluctant to send anyone or any *thing* there if he did not have to. And the creature *had* been placed under his care. The chance to reform a damned soul appealed to his sense of fun and adventure and gave him a chance to poke a figurative finger in the many eyes of the so-called Masters of the Pit.

"Very well," he said, "Come along."

"You are the master. I am your servant. How shall I be called?" she had asked.

To avoid complications his answer was "Felicia Baker." Then he gave her his first commands.

"You will do no evil. You will commit no sin, break no law, or bring harm to any person – unless I tell you to. Is that understood?"

"Yes,Master."

"Call me Simon. You're no genie and I'm not an astronaut. And finally, you are to always act in my best interest."

"Yes … Simon."

"You will live with me so I can keep an eye on you. Other than that, you can make your own choices."

Felicia's first choice was to call herself "Fel."

"I made a mistake once, betrayed the Three, and fell a long way. My name will remind me of my fate should I give you cause to return me to the Pit."

Fel's second choice was to leave the spare bedroom Simon had given her and join him in his bed.

Simon was, or had once been, only human. He eagerly accepted Fel's choice.

Sleep was not the only thing new to Fel. Simon was an experienced teacher. She proved to be an enthusiastic student.

It was a week after Fel had moved in. A week spent in arranging the affairs of the person the law believed to be Felicia Baker. Simon was reading a collection of stories about space-going bartenders when Fel came over to him.

"You know that one day I will betray you."

"What makes you say that?" Simon asked, no longer interested in a galaxy made of nothing but ethanol.

"I betrayed the Names when I rebelled. I betrayed the Dark Ones when I seized the chance to escape the Pit. And so one day I will betray you. It is in my nature."

Simon thought back to the tale of the Scorpion, who had stung the tortoise knowing it would bring doom to both. Having always been more of a hare than a tortoise, Simon smiled said, "Then we will have to make sure that doesn't happen."

As Simon watched Fel sleeping he reflected that that conversation had occurred more than a month ago, and so far she had adapted, embracing her mostly human state and showing no signs of plotting any treason against him. Unless it was to co-opt the affections of Kitty.

Kitty was a small boa constrictor that had attached itself to Simon (first literally than figuratively) during an adventure in Belize. The story of how he had smuggled her into the States was one he told often, but never the same way twice. When Fel moved in Kitty had almost immediately transferred her affections to the woman. Simon frequently awoke to find the boa wrapped lovingly around Fel's naked body, a sight he found both disturbing and erotic.

But there was no Kitty that day. The snake had recently swallowed a nice juicy rat and was somewhere digesting her meal. Simon did not expect to see her for at least a few days.

With Fel still asleep, Simon was enjoying breakfast when his cell phone rang, its caller ID informing him that Detective Caitlin Hood of the Baltimore Police Department Homicide Unit wanted to talk.

With the prospect of some new adventure in the offing, Simon answered with a "Katie, how nice of you to call. Who's dead and other than confessing how can I help?"

"Tombs," Hood said in a most serious tone, "I'm downstairs.

Can I come up?"

"Of course, I'll buzz you in. Just give me a few minutes to dress. Unless of course you'd rather I didn't."

"I can wait. Please dress."

"Your loss."

Ten minutes later Simon opened his door to the detective. He had just offered her coffee when Fel walked into the living room.

At least she dressed for company this time, Simon thought, remembering a recently delivered pizza. The eyeful that Domino's man had gotten was such that he had left without his tip. "Dressed" however, was a relative concept and to Fel it meant a sleep shirt that was just long enough for modesty but wouldn't be if for any reason she raised her arms over her head.

Despite having lived and slept with the woman for some time, Simon could not help but stare. He was still amazed at her unnatural beauty. So apparently was Caitlin Hood.

Simon caught the detective looking at Fel for longer than simple curiosity would explain. Understanding the situation, he gave her another minute before saying, "Fel, dear, perhaps it might be better, for all of us, if you were to get fully dressed."

"Of course, Simon," Fel said in apparent innocence, then smiled in such a way as to give the lie to appearances. She was, after all, a demon, and it was her nature to discern a mortal's desires and exploit them for her own amusement. As she turned and walked toward the bedroom two pairs of eyes followed until she was out of sight.

"Well," Simon said, "let's have that coffee now. It's Zeke's Tell Tale Dark. Just the way to start a day."

"And now you know," Hood said once Simon had poured the coffee and set out pastries from the Woodlea Bakery. The detective was clearly worried that Simon now knew a secret part of her personal life.

"My knowing changes nothing, Katie. I am not one for gossip, unless it's salacious and about someone I don't like. But I am comforted to know the reason why you have consistently refused all of my indecent proposals. I was afraid it was me."

Hood took a sip of her coffee before replying. "Oh, it was you, Tombs. I'm gay but can be tempted. Trust me, it's you."

"A hit, Detective Hood, a very palpable hit. I think it is time you started calling me Simon. Now tell me all about this horrible crime for which you need my help."

Despite needing Simon's help, Detective Hood hesitated. She had long had her suspicions about him but had taken no steps to confirm them. Now she had no choice. Feeling that she was about to walk deeply into very dark woods in which there lurked unheavenly creatures and from which there might be no return, Hood said, "I need your ... expert opinion."

"About?"

"You'll understand when we get there."

"Very well, but I would like to bring Fel."

"She seems very young."

"Yes, she does. But trust me, Fel is older than she appears. Much, much older. And in some things she is more expert than I."

Fel chose that moment to emerge, fully and modestly dressed. "Well then, shall we be off?" Simon asked. "Fel, you're coming with us. It seems that the game is afoot."

The scene was an abandoned building, a former Catholic school off Orleans St, not too far from police headquarters. Crime scene tape surrounded it and all four of Baltimore's TV stations were waiting outside for some word of what had happened and who had been killed, hoping that it was someone important and that they'd find out in time for the noon news.

Hood had driven. From the back seat came, "Oh good, the circus is in town." Simon's past activities had given him a small measure of notoriety. And while his fifteen minutes had expired years ago any recognition might possibly renew the media's interest.

Hood shrugged and said, "Nothing to be done." She'd been working murders long enough to learn how to ignore the media when she could and use them when she must.

It was the way Simon asked "No?" that made the detective think that she should have driven around to the back of the school. As an officer lifted the yellow tape for her car to pass and TV cameras were trained on her car, a commotion nearing panic broke out around the news trucks.

"It appears that their recording devices have suddenly stopped working and that they've lost their live feed. Right now they are broadcasting nothing but static," Simon said as if he had had nothing to do with it.

The three quickly made their way from the car to the school entrance, Hood muttering and already questioning her decision to seek Simon's help while at the same time wishing she knew how to do whatever it was he just did.

The crime scene was in the basement. It was, as Simon expected, a homicide, with the victim bound to an inverted cross that had been firmly bolted into the unpainted cinderblock of an exterior wall.

Present were two uniformed officers, one at the foot of the stairs which the three had descended and the other standing close to a door to the outside. Another officer was outside the door. Two detectives were standing around watching a young woman with a Crime Scene Science patch on the shoulder of her uniform shirt wave some kind of three-bladed device out of Star Trek around the crucified man.

"She's scanning the body," Hood explained. "From her scan she'll create a 3D image of the victim."

"And they call what I do magic," Simon muttered *sotto voce*. Out loud he said, "Caitlin, don't you think it is a bit crowded in here for what you want me need me for, whatever that is?"

"Everybody out!" Hood shouted in a tone that brooked no argument. The officers and detective were quick to obey. The woman from the crime lab calmly and quietly worked at finishing her scan, earning Simon's silent approval. Only when she was done did she make her exit, leaving Hood, Simon, and Fel alone but only after warning them not to touch anything.

"What do you think?" she asked Simon.

Much like the crime scene investigator, Simon took his time, looking at the body from all angles, building his own 3D image in his mind.

The victim had been securely tied to the cross, with ropes around his ankles and wrist firmly holding him in place. The spikes through his feet and palms weren't needed, just an added cruelty. From the bleeding that had occurred, it was clear that the deceased had been crucified while still alive.

Death had been long in coming, and had occurred not long ago. Insect activity had just begun and Simon detected only a whiff of decomposition.

He had seen worse but long ago and in foreign and now forgotten lands.

"At first glance, Caitlin, I would guess that someone didn't like old Pete very much."

"Old Pete! You mean you know him?"

"Never laid eyes on him before. Of course, his name could be Rocky, or the Rock, or even Cephas, not that anyone uses that name anymore. I do hope it's not Simon."

Despite the Homicide Unit's unofficial motto of "We Work for God" Caitlin Hood was not a very religious person. She had seen too much death and suffering in her career to believe in a kind and compassionate Savior and prayed to a just and vengeful God only when the occasion called for it, which in Baltimore was too damned often.

"St. Peter," she said as the story of the apostle came back to her.

"No denying it. Now, what do you need to know?"

"When I, we saw the upside down cross we started thinking black mass or some other kind of Satanic rite. Could that have occurred here?'

Simon looked around. Other than the inverted hanged man there was nothing of ritual in the basement. Nor did he get a sense that the Tarot was involved. He had, however, brought an expert on things demonic so why not use her.

"Fel, what do you think?'

Fel slowly approached the body. She seemed at war with herself, not wishing to get too close to the holy symbol yet drawn to the unholy death.

"It's okay," Simon assured her. "You're with me. Nothing will hurt or come for you. And you needn't fear the cross. You're working for the good guys now."

Only then did Fel get close, closer than Simon had. She took her time examining the body and the cross.

"Is she ... sniffing?" Hood asked.

"Probably."

"One day you'll have to tell me how you two met."

"You really don't want me to, and you wouldn't believe me if I did."

Finally, Fel finished her examination. "There was no summoning. No one tried to bring anything over. But there was Evil done." The way Fel said it, both Simon and Hood could hear the capital in the word. Fel went on, "But is not direct. It is Evil working from a distance. And I sense... there have been others."

"Others," Hood asked, correctly assuming that this single, bizarre murder was about to spin out of control. "In this building?"

Fel paused, expanded her senses. There was an as yet undiscovered body in the foundation of the building, and there had been two knifings and one suicide some years ago, but these were all the result of human action. There was nothing like the ... odor of Evil coming from the hanged man.

"No," she said, "not here. But elsewhere, before this and possibly after."

"More crucifixions?"

"No, Ma...Simon. More killing of saints."

"What did she mean 'more killing of saints'?" Hood asked Simon once the three of them were at Police Headquarters. Hood had picked them up at the basement entrance, which opened on an alley, the access to which was controlled by the BPD. She didn't want Simon causing another news blackout. Once might have been a coincidence. Twice and the media would report that the BPD had some way of blocking their transmissions.

To Simon's surprise, the detective commandeered her sergeant's office. It made a nice change from the interview rooms in which she had questioned him the last two, no three times he'd been there. Fel had been excluded from their conference, being seated at a detective's cubicle where Hood could keep one eye on Simon while watching her with the other.

And watch her she did. Despite trying not to, Hood's attention kept wandering towards the beautiful, young, and possibly dangerous woman outside the office.

"The killing of saints," Simon replied in answer to her question. "I believe that someone is symbolically attacking martyrs, recreating their deaths for some purpose of his own. What that purpose might be, well, you can ask him when you catch him."

Simon said this with an air of finality, as if his job was over.

"Will you be helping us?" Hood asked, a part of her sensing that this case might be beyond human jurisdiction and another not wanting to lose contact with the woman outside the office.

"Of course, Caitlin, you can call me if you need me but…" He looked out at Fel. "She's on the edge of a very sharp knife, balanced between the Light and the Dark. So far I'm keeping her balanced but a push at the wrong time and she might…I might have to do something I really don't want to."

Simon stood to leave. "I'll get you a ride home," Hood offered.

"Don't bother, Caitlin. These days I always seem to have the correct change for the bus."

"What do we do next?" Fel asked Simon once the two were back in his apartment.

"We sit back and watch a movie, something fun with a lot of singing and dancing."

"No, I mean about the murdered saints. What will we do to help them?"

"Why do you care?" Simon replied gently.

"Below, we always knew when one of *them* died. The Masters rejoiced that one of *Their* servants had been killed horribly. I too rejoiced because another's pain, any pain, reduced ours for just a moment. But you are now my master and you have told me that I am one of the good guys. So I must keep pain from happening. How will we do this?"

"For now, we do nothing." At the look of confusion on Fel's

face Simon explained. "First the police will do their job. And then, if needed, we will do ours. In the meantime,"

Looking through his extensive movie collection, Simon pulled out a DVD. "Here we go, *That's Entertainment.*"

"What's entertainment?"

"This is."

Fel enjoyed the review of MGM's best musical numbers so much that Simon put in Part II. When that was over they went into the bedroom where they made their own music.

I just had to call him, Caitlin Hood said to herself as the search to identify other possible victims of what might be Baltimore's newest serial killer began. Her sergeant, his lieutenant, and the major who ruled over all of Homicide were not entirely convinced of the killer's existence, especially since the source came from the ethically questionable Simon Tombs and his "ditzy, body-sniffing girlfriend." However, given the manner of death of their one victim and the fact that his first name really was Peter, they had to allow for the possibility. So they assigned Detective Hood some help – a detective whose closure rate was so low that his absence on the street would not be missed, two uniformed officers currently on light duty due to on-the-job injuries, and a police cadet waiting for the next academy class to start.

They focused on unsolved murders, eliminating those who had been killed with firearms or did not have a recognizable martyr's name. Then they compared the causes of death with their namesake martyr's demise.

They found three strong candidates and one possible. They rejected the trainee's argument that a drug overdose victim named Stephen be included "because he was stoned when he died."

Once they had their possible victims the real police work began. The small task force looked for common threads between the victims, the crime scenes and the evidence. They found … nothing.

"There's no common thread," Hood told Simon over drinks at Sebastian's. "There's nothing that ties any one of the victims to any other. On each scene or body there are prints and DNA that don't belong to the victim. But the prints and DNA are different on each scene and none have hit on AFIS or CODIS. Other than the fact that each victim was found in a remote area, there's nothing. My lieutenant is pulling the plug."

"These victims, who were they and how did they die?"

"A man named Saul was found beheaded in Leakin Park. At first, we thought animals had been responsible, the body was that far gone. But the ME took a closer look and found the cut marks. A woman named Joan was burned to death in a car just east of Armistead Gardens. The body of a man named Mark was fished from the harbor. There was enough of him left to show what the ME called fatal road rash."

"St. Mark, dragged to death. St. Joan, burned alive. St. Paul aka Saul, beheaded. Anyone else?"

"That's it. We thought a woman named Agnes was one of them. She'd been stabbed in the throat and left in a vacant house. But last night her ex bragged about doing her to a girl he was trying to impress. She dimed him out."

"So that makes four so far."

"No, Simon, that makes, according to my bosses, an incredible coincidence. And I'm not sure they're wrong. Given the number of murders in Baltimore, I'm sure I could make a case for any number of them being somehow related to each other. Your girlfriend might be as beautiful as an angel from Heaven but what she sniffed wasn't evil, it was body rot."

"Caitlin, you're not that far off about her being an angel from Above, but you're wrong about the rest. There will be more deaths – people beheaded, shot with arrows, or thrown from windows then beaten, and more crucifixions. Any further deaths will not only be on our killer but on you and me as well. And that is not a burden I'm willing to accept."

"You're not going to let this go, are you?" Simon shook his head. "It's going to end badly for someone, isn't it?"

"Hopefully the killer."

"Damn it. What do you need, Simon?"

"First of all, another drink. Then the locations of the other four deaths."

"You mean three deaths."

"I mean four. Throw in Agnes as a control. Magic and science have many of the same rules." Simon had his drink then stood, left enough money on the table to cover the bill and a generous tip. "Now if you'll forgive, Fel is at home trying to cook. I have to get back before she burns my building to the ground."

Detective Hood came through. A messenger delivered a packet containing the details of all five murders. *Clever, Caitlin*, Simon thought. *We can each honestly say that I did not receive anything from you.* He began his work.

"You can't!" Fel shouted when Simon told her what he was going to do. "I just escaped the Pit. Why would you be willing to go there? What if they come after you?"

"They won't. They don't dare. Not yet. And when they do I'll be ready for them. And I must go. The Evil that you sensed, we don't know what it is. I may need the power I get from releasing repentant souls from damnation."

"Releasing them to where?"

A question Simon had asked himself each time he had done this. "To Paradise or oblivion. I'm not quite sure."

Fel was silent for a moment. "If I asked, would you grant me such release?"

It was a question Simon did not know how to answer. Finally, he said, "I would not begrudge you Paradise. But I would not want to lose you to oblivion. Still, if ever the time is right, I will try. But now, I need to be alone."

Fel left him. As he had several times before, Simon sat back in his chair, his mind picturing a cord. The cord became a rope, the rope became a bridge, and it was over this bridge Simon walked into Hell.

Damned souls flocked around him. Some few shone brightly. Simon selected the brightest one. He did not know what sins had condemned the soul to eternal torment, only that now, after what might have been days, years, or centuries, the soul was truly repentant. He offered the Choice and the Choice was accepted. As the now freed soul faded from Hell, Simon turned back to the bridge. As he was crossing it he heard a voice that came from nowhere and everywhere. It called him by a name he had not used since the Fifties.

"One day, the rope will fray and the bridge will break. Yours will be a long fall into the Deep Pit."

"One day, perhaps, if the Word so wills it." Simon felt the Pit creature recoil from his use of one of the Names. "But not today."

Simon woke, his being filled with power.

Midnight to some was the witching hour, the time when the old day flowed into the new. To Simon, it was just another tick of the clock. Evening and dawn, those were the two periods during which the Light and the Dark meet, times when the opposing forces were balanced, neither having the advantage over the other. Simon preferred the dawn, when the darkness was at its weakest but not yet gone.

But it was at midnight that he and Fel returned to the school. He did not know how long they would be, and the lateness of the hour made it likely that they would be undisturbed. As for the forces of darkness, that's why he had brought Fel.

The police were done with it as a scene – the yellow tape was gone and the doors were locked. The latter was not a problem; Simon had a way with doors and locks.

Of the five deaths, this was the newest scene, the others stretching back months, the first being just a few days after Simon had returned from Assateague Island with Fel. As the newest site, the place where Peter Wallace had met his end would be the easiest for him to read.

"What do you want me to do?" Fel asked Simon as he sat in against the wall from which the cross had been removed.

"Stand watch. Keep me safe. Do what you must against anyone or any thing that tries to harm me."

"What I must." There was a world of meaning in Fel's acknowledgment all of which Simon understood and some of which worried him. He closed his eyes, trying not to think that he was putting his trust in a fallen angel who had once said she would betray him.

Violent death leaves an unseen but tangible stain. Simon sought it, found it, and began working backwards from the moment of Peter's death, feeling first the prolonged agony of the man's death. Next came pain of the nails, spikes actually, driven into his wrists and feet. Then came Peter's return to consciousness and his disorientation from awakening upside down.

An inverted view of his killer who was holding a mallet in his hand.

A description for Caitlin, Simon thought, *although not a good one.*

He turned attention back to Peter. He had been in an Inner Harbor parking garage when a blow from behind rendered him unconscious.

In his mind, Simon again followed the chain of events, this time forward to Peter's brief glimpse of the killer.

Simon went deeper into his trance, deeper into what had been the scene. He sensed the Evil that Fel had detected. It seemed to be around the blonde man and in him, but not of him. No matter. He had his man, he had his essence. He could find him.

Simon woke to find Fel standing protectively near his body. Moaning came from a corner of the basement.

"What happened?" he asked.

"You forgot to lock the door behind you. Two men came in. They saw you, they decided to rob you. They did not see me."

"And?"

"They will live. They are more frightened than injured."

"What did you ... no, don't tell me. Let's just go home. There's still work to be done."

On their way back to the apartment, Simon telephoned Detective Hood.

"This better be good. I'm off duty and not alone."

"My apologies to you and to whomever you're with. Your killer is a white male in his mid-thirties, tall, blonde, well-muscled. Unless you've found it or it's been towed or stolen, Peter Wallace's car is in the Harbor Park Garage. Good enough?"

Despite her now having to leave a warm bed in which was a warm companion, Hood agreed that it was good enough.

Back in his apartment, Simon was forgoing his own warm bed with an even warmer companion. As Fel slept, Simon was in his study, a large map of the city covering the desk before him. With a finger on the location of the old school, he closed his eyes and recalled the trace of evil and the essence of the killer.

His finger moved south and west on the map. It paused slightly as it crossed where the Harbor Park garage was then continued on, stopping only a few blocks away on the spot marking a Water Street condo tower.

He wanted to stop there, to call Hood back and tell her where to find her man. To leave it to the police to find one man in a building full of people. But there were other scenes and he wanted to be sure.

Simon lifted his finger from the map, placed it on the site of Joan Rollins's murder. Again he recalled the essence of the blonde killer, expecting his finger to move south and west toward Water Street. Instead, it remained where it was. There was no connection between Peter Wallace's killer and Joan's death.

The next night found him in Herring Run Park, just east of the community of Armistead Gardens. Roads ran into the woods. It was on a trail off one of these roads that a charred patch of ground marked the place where a burned out car containing Joan's body was found. There was, according to the autopsy report, no doubt that she had burned to death.

Joan had been killed a week before Peter. Again Fel watched over Simon as he sat on the now cold earth and went back to when the earth was not so cold, when it felt the heat of a car on fire above it.

He concentrated on the fire and from that on the woman who had been killed.

He felt the intense pain that caused her to black out when her body could take no more. He felt her despair on waking up bound in a burning car with no means of escape. A blow to her head while walking to her car from a store at Canton Crossing.

Joan had met her death in her own car. Her killer had driven it to this site. Simon sought him next.

There was the same touch of Evil that he and Fel he had sensed in the school. There was, however, no trace of the blonde man. The same Evil, a different killer. A cult perhaps, a new one which required its initiates to symbolically murder a saint. He hoped that was the case. He did not want to think about the alternative.

The touch of Evil was stronger this time, despite being a week older. Maybe the killer stayed to enjoy his work, to watch a woman burn to death. Or else Joan's quicker, fiery death left a greater imprint on the scene.

Simon thought about going back to his study, to his map, attempting to track the Evil to its source. But there it would be weaker. Here it was strong.

Fel, again I place my trust in you, he thought. He called on the power he had within him, brought up his memory of the map, and drew in the essence of the Evil.

The map blazed in his mind as a scarlet path was drawn from where he was sitting to a townhome on Boston Street just at the foot of Linwood Ave. This killer lived there and since "there" was a single family dwelling he would be easy to find.

The mage did not stop there. He forced the path to extend to the other scenes, to Leakin Park where Saul Kinney was beheaded and from there to a home in Dickeyville. He felt the Evil then. It became a more solid presence, fighting him, trying to keep him from the pier of the old BGE plant where Mark Roberson's body was found.

More power. Simon's head throbbing as he sought to track the Evil to its primary source. But it had power of its own, and retreated, gave way, and vanished. This allowed Simon to connect the final threads, to that stretch of Annapolis Road where Mark was dragged to death behind a Chevy pickup.

The throbbing on his head grew worse. His brief mental conflict with the Evil and his forcing his will on the mystic plane had taken him to the limits of his power. And there was still more to do. From

Annapolis Road, the path led to a large house in Linthicum. He then tried to extend the thread to where Agnes Benjamin was stabbed and barely managed to confirm that her death was not involved before he passed out.

He awoke in darkness, not quite sure where he was. Heaven? Hell? Or a special Limbo prepared for those who lived on the grey edge between the Light and Dark. Then something cold, long, and smooth squeezed him in its gentle embrace and he knew he was home.

"Nice to see you too, Kitty," he said. As the snake shared his body heat something occurred to him. "So that's why you prefer her. She does burn hotter than I do."

The bedroom door opened, proving enough light for him to see his rescuer. "Thank you, Fel," he said, disentangling himself from Kitty. "How did you get me home?"

"Carried you to the car and drove you home."

"But you don't know how to drive."

"She did, so I do," Fel replied in a rare reference to the first Felicia Baker. "And do not think to cross the bridge again anytime soon. You would be easy prey."

"Good advice. Natural talent aided by guile and deceit it is. Thank you again."

"Just looking out for your best interest … Master."

"None of the four have records, Simon," Detective Hood told him. They were again at Sebastian's, this time accompanied by Fel. The young woman was sitting closer to Hood than to Simon, who did not seem to mind. "Not even a speeding ticket among them. And since psychic tracing is neither a recognized forensic technique nor an acceptable investigatory tool, there's no way we can get a warrant for these four."

Hood held up the list Simon had given her. It contained the names and addresses of the four people he had traced some nights before.

"I don't understand," Fel said, moving in a closer to the detective. "We have told you who helped commit these murders and where to find them. Why can't you?"

Hood moved her chair away from the young woman. "Where are you from?" she asked abruptly. She'd banter with Tombs, but not with his sidekick.

"Someplace where they would be punished harshly and for a long time."

"Fel, dear, would you please leave Caitlin and me alone. Order another Pepper Special then make those calls I asked you to."

"Yes, Ma…Simon."

"Pepper Special?" Hood asked.

"Yes. Dr. Pepper mixed with Sagamore Rye. Fel likes it but I don't think it will catch on. But to the matter at hand. What if our four suspects …"

"Your four suspects."

"These four suspects," Simon indicated the list, "what if the BPD obtained their DNA legitimately as a result of its investigation into a series of burglaries, robberies, and/or non-fatal assaults? Or what if you just walked away from this. If you do I promise that this killing of the saints will end. It will be messy but it will stop. Your choice."

What have I done? Hood asked herself. Then she looked at the smiling man sitting across the table from her. *Who are you, Simon Tombs? What are you?* She was very much afraid that she would not like the answers to those questions. Hood looked over the list.

Dora Newton – Linthicum.

Clark Sellers – Water Street.

Jeremy Leach – Dickeyville.

Krista Greenwood – Canton

These four were far from the usual suspects, the kind Hood and her associates could drag off the streets based on the word of a real or imagined "confidential informant" and held for a pleasant chat without charges being filed or lawyers getting in the way. During the discussion, drinks would be provided and smoking allowed. Once the suspects had denied any knowledge of whatever crime was on the table, of any crime in fact, they would be allowed to leave. Rides home would be offered but likely turned down least their neighbors get the wrong idea about their level of cooperation with the police.

Once the suspects and left, their abandoned soda cans, water bottles, and cigarette butts would be gathered up, submitted to evidence, swabbed for DNA, and dusted for prints. And the Great Wheel of Justice would continue to turn.

No, the four citizens on Tombs's list would speed dial their attorneys on the way to the Homicide Unit. On behalf of their clients, these attorneys, would decline any comment and refuse any offers of hospitality. Hood even knew of one who kept antiseptic wipes in her briefcase and would clean whatever areas her clients might have touched.

Bringing them in was not an option. Nor was allowing Tombs to commit several felonies, up to and possibly including homicide, with her implicit consent. That wasn't how the law, her law, worked.

"There is, of course, one other option," she heard Simon say.

"What is it?" she asked, sure she would not like the answer.

Her calls finished, Fel returned to the table. "They'll be here."

"All of them?"

"Greenwood was reluctant but quickly came around."

"Tombs, what have you done?"

"Now, Caitlin, I thought you were going to call me Simon. And I've done nothing but lay out unacceptable scenarios. Fel here did all the work. At my request, she called each of our persons of interest and invited them here on Saturday morning. Prior to the invitation, she described each of their crimes, including details that only the killer, or someone who witnessed the killing, would know. She also threatened to provide these details to that scandal rag *The Baltimore Truth* if they didn't show up."

"And you think they will?"

"Of course. Legal proof is one thing, being convicted in the media is a life sentence, innocence and guilt be damned. Besides, I doubt whoever is behind this would approve. His kind thrives on secrecy."

"Who are we talking about here? You mean to say there's someone else?"

"Of course. These four are puppets. Someone else is pulling their strings. And on Saturday morning I'll know who it is."

"We'll know who it is. I plan on being there."

Simon was uncharacteristically quiet for several minutes. His face darkened. Finally, "Caitlin, Detective Hood. I would strongly advise against that. There are paths in life down which the average person should not go. A long time ago I set foot on one of those paths and said goodbye to a great deal of what you'd call normal. Let Fel and me make this journey. We'll bring you back souvenirs like signed confessions and closed cases."

"It's my case, Mr. Tombs. I'll be there."

"Your Choice, Detective. May you be happy with it."

Come Saturday morning Simon's suspects entered Sebastian's one by one. Krista Greenwood was the first. She was fifteen minutes early and sat in a booth against the wall as if waiting for someone to come take her order. It was much too early for that, Sebastian's did not do breakfast, or even brunch. Simon let her sit there and worry.

Jeremy Leach was next, just slightly ahead of Dora Newton. He held the door for her, allowing her to enter first. He went straight to Simon's tables. She hung back, looked toward Greenwood then joined Leach.

Clark Sellers was five minutes late. He strode in as if this was a party and he the guest of honor. *In a way,* Simon thought, *it is and he is, one of them at least.*

Three tables were arranged so that the suspects could sit four abreast, all facing Simon. Sellers claimed the center spot, between Leach and Newton.

"Please come join us, Ms. Greenwood," Simon said. As she walked over he thought to himself that none of them looked anything but average, that other than higher than normal bank balances there was nothing to distinguish them from people who had not committed murder.

Fel was sitting next to Simon. Detective Hood was off to the side, an observer only. Simon did not introduce either one. Nor did he say his name.

"Let's get on with it," grumbled Sellers, as if there was something more important that his life and freedom.

"Very well," Simon said. "I won't offer you drinks nor will I thank the four of you for coming. This is not a social occasion. You four are here under coercion, your alternatives being the police or the press."

He carefully looked at each one of them. "St. Paul, St. Joan, St. Peter, and St. Mark." he let that set in then, "Or should I say, Saul Kinney, Joan Rollins, Peter Wallace, and Mark Roberson. I know what you did. I want to know why and for whom."

There was a silence, one Simon did nothing to relieve as he looked at one after the other, looking past their eyes and into their souls and seeing the fear there – fear of him, fear of what they had done, fear that there was no way out on either side of death. But right then they feared someone else more than him.

As Simon had expected, Sellers broke first. "I don't have to stay and listen to this crap." He stood to go.

"Then leave," Simon said. "No one will stop you, any of you. Leave and be damned. But you leave behind your only chance at redemption."

At "redemption" he felt a slight hope emanate from the three still sitting. Sellers hesitated then sat back down.

"You were, each of you, offered something. Money, power, revenge, the best sex you ever had, the real answer to life, the universe, and everything. It's doesn't matter what and I don't care. What I want to know is what you gave up in exchange. Please tell me it was something more than your souls, for you lost them the second you said yes to this mess."

Leach wanted to answer, so did Newton. The other two were unsure. No one spoke, their fear overcoming the faint bit of hope he had offered them. So it was time to make them more afraid.

"You don't seem to understand. You sold yourself to something evil and unless you repent, I mean truly repent and make things right, when you die you will go to Hell. Unfortunately, these days most people don't believe in Hell, or they joke about it, or they make up stories about it. There are no heroes in hell, my friends, only damned souls, fallen demons, and suffering, eternal suffering. But I can see you don't believe me."

Simon let out a long sigh. "Show them, Fel."

"But …"

"Just a glimpse, Fel. It may save their souls."

Entering their minds the way Simon had taught her, Fel opened herself up to the four. Countless millennia ago, when there was still a Garden, she had betrayed the Three. For that she had suffered pain that the human mind could barely comprehend. She let less than a second of that pain touch the minds of the people in front of her.

Greenwood and Leach screamed, long sustained cries that would leave their throats sore for days. Newton just sat there, lost to the world. Sellers wept openly.

Ten minutes, then fifteen. By twenty the four had somewhat recovered. Their faces were ashen, Leach's hair had a white streak that would never leave him. Tears still ran down Sellers's cheeks. And all of them were more afraid then they had ever been in their lives.

"What did you give up?" Simon said quietly and gently.

"A week of my life," Sellers said. "I was conscious the whole time while … he … hunted and killed that man."

"Three days, and the same," Leach confessed.

"One night, one horrible night," said Newton.

"A day and a night," sobbed Greenwood. "He … made me watch her burn."

"Who is he?" Simon asked in a whisper.

Each one gave the same name – Weston Ellis.

"I wish I could say that your sins are forgiven you, to go and sin no more. But you will have to forgive yourselves, only then might Heaven will show its Mercy. But for your penance," Simon waved Hood over. "This is Detective Caitlin Hood. She will read you your rights. You will waive them, then you will give her a full confession as to what you did. You will omit any mention of your possession, just that you were members of a cult led by this Weston Ellis. Caitlin, can you handle these four from here."

Hood was visibly shaken. She knew something terrible had happened to the four but wasn't sure what. She was sure that she did not want to know. She nodded and called her unit for some help. Then she asked Simon,

"What about this Weston Eilis?"

"He's mine."

"Like hell he is."

"Caitlin, he is exactly like Hell. Which is why you need to leave him to me."

"To us," Fel corrected.

"Simon, you told me earlier that, what did you call it, the path I walk is my choice. Well, I choose to see it through, whatever the cost. This Ellis is responsible for four deaths that we know of. It's my job to bring him in. I choose that path years ago and I'll stay on it."

Knowing the name the one behind the killing of the saints was using, and having touched his essence more than once, Simon had little trouble in locating Weston Ellis. A night of concertation in his study, his mental focus on the map of the city and Simon's finger was dragged from each murder scene to the same apartment building off Boston St.

How disappointing, he thought, *that my opponent has chosen to live near a travel plaza and a truck stop.* But then he remembered some of the places he had lived and reminded himself not to take Ellis lightly.

"It's too soon to cross the bridge," he told Fel when she asked him about his preparations. "The Pit Lords are probably aware of what is happening and have no doubt laid their snares."

"This Ellis may be one of those snares, Simon."

"He may be, or he could be an inspired amateur hoping to impress. Poor damned fool if he is. But I've faced his kind in the past with just guile, cunning, and charm, and God willing I'll be able to do so after tonight."

"You have more than that … Master."

"Yes, I do. I have you, my dear Fel. Now if you would be so kind as to call Caitlin and tell her to meet us at the McDonalds near the Travel Plaza. There's nothing like a Big Mac before facing the forces of Evil."

Simon knocked on the door of Apartment 2B. The man who

answered was nothing special, not outwardly at least. He wore jeans and a polo shirt with a store logo on the left side of the chest. He was barefoot and his brown going to grey hair was uncombed. Not quite the face of Evil Simon had imagined.

But beneath Weston Ellis's unimpressive facade Simon could feel the power the man had gathered from damning four weak souls and symbolically murdering four saints. It radiated from the man like the heat from a sun lamp and Simon was very much aware of the danger of being badly burned.

"Mr. Ellis," Simon said politely, "I believe you have been expecting us. May we come in?"

"I was expecting someone. Please come in. I'd offer you a seat but ..."

Simon, Hood, and Fel looked around. There was no place to sit, the chairs and sofa being covered with the debris from a lonely man living a lonely life.

"Not to worry. I think we all prefer to stand. I am ..."

"You are Simon Tombs." Looking toward Hood Ellis said, "I suspect this one is from the police." He looked at Fel. "And this creature is yours I believe."

Fel bristled. Before she could react further Simon said, "Ms. Baker is not your concern. Now as to why we're here ..."

"I know why you're here, Tombs. I read the papers, watch the news. The police arrested four people in reference to a murder cult."

"Which you were behind. They all mentioned your name."

"Prove it," Ellis challenged. "Arrest me and prove it," he dared Hood. "There is no proof that these four worked together, conspired together, or even knew each other before you brought them together. And please, try explaining my involvement to any judge and jury. Try getting them to believe that I possessed these people and used their bodies to commit these crimes."

"I would not dream of doing so. Neither would Detective Hood. We were hoping, however, that you would confess to being the head of the cult and agree to a lengthy prison term during which you could contemplate your sins and work towards your redemption."

Ellis started to laugh, a long, loud laugh in which none of the other three joined in. When he was done,

"Very funny, Tombs, but I think I'll decline. But here's my offer. I will continue to use the weak and the greedy to kill the people of Baltimore. And no matter how many of my puppets you find and arrest, you will never connect any of them to me. And still more will die."

"Unless …" Simon prompted.

Ellis smiled in triumph. "I was on Assateague Island that night you interrupted our sacrifice, the night this," he indicated Fel, "came through instead. I stayed behind when the others ran. I saw her crawl off the altar. I heard her call you 'Master.' I want her. I want her power. Together with my own, I'll have everything I want – fame, wealth, and women. And when I have it all, I'll trade her back to the Pit for a place of honor and glory."

Poor damned fool, Simon thought again. Then added, *poor fools us*. He knew he dare not physically confront Ellis. The man's power was too great. Hood would be no help. She was constrained by her duty. That left Fel.

Simon thought of the scorpion and its nature. He hoped that Fel would understand. There really was no other choice and never had been.

Simon sighed, as if in defeat. "My dear Fel, I truly regret this." The young woman's face paled at the betrayal she saw coming. "Please stand by Mr. Ellis."

She did so, saying "Yes, Master."

"Remember my first commands to you?"

"Yes, Master," she said again.

"Then do what you must. Be true to your nature."

For a second her eyes widened, asking Simon if he was sure. Another second, a quick nod yes. In the third second, Weston Ellis realized that something was wrong. In the fourth second, his dreams of fame, wealth, and women faded away as Fel rammed her fist through his back.

Her hand emerged from his chest, holding Ellis's beating heart. Surprisingly he was still alive, his power sustaining his life.

"You damned fool," Simon said. "You will be going to Hell, but sooner than you planned. There the Masters of the Pit will not take any notice of you, or what you think you've done for them. There will be no power, no glory, and no honor. There will only be you and endless suffering. Think on that as you burn forever. Release him, Fel."

Fel removed her hand. As she did so Ellis's chest and back closed up and he collapsed on the floor.

It had happened all too fast for Catlin Hood. First Simon was confronting their suspect, seemingly getting him to confess. Then they were making some deal. Then the girl Fel, the one Hood had found herself dreaming about even as she lay next to another, she …

Simon looked down at the body. "An autopsy will show that Weston Ellis died of a heart attack, one he had just after confessing to his role in the cult killings."

For a moment all was silent as Hood tried to take in what had just happened. Finally,

"You two should go," Hood said flatly. "I have to call this in and you should not be here." As Simon nodded his agreement Hood added, "And don't call me, Tombs, not for anything. I don't think I want to know you anymore."

"I understand," Simon said. "But remember, Caitlin Hood, it was by your Choice that now you know what we are. And you can never unknow it. I hope you will forgive us, and yourself."

After Simon and Fel left her alone, Detective Hood looked at the dead man on the floor. Having seen how he had actually died, she knew that she would continue to have dreams about the girl. They would not be the erotic dreams where the two of them entwined their bodies and pleasured each other. No, she knew that when she dreamed of Fel she would always see the girl's hand emerging from a man's chest.

Back in their apartment, Simon said, "Fel, about what I had you do …"

"I did what was needed. Neither you nor I had a choice. It was what our natures demanded."

Having said this, Fel went to her own room and did not come to Simon's bed for several nights after.

Guardian Demon

Simon Tombs sat on the balcony of his apartment and stared into the night sky. There wasn't much of it to be seen, just the space above a four-story hotel that sat between two taller buildings. Still, this bit of starry blackness relaxed him. As he wondered what might lay beyond it his somewhat-reformed demon companion joined him.

Sitting in the chair next to him Fel said, "That woman Jillian called again."

"What did she want?"

"She said not to get involved in the Snow Queen case, whatever that is."

"Fel, if she or anyone from her office calls back please tell her that I want nothing to do with that story." Simon turned his attention back to what he regarded as his small piece of the sky. "Now if you'll excuse me, I'd like to get back to contemplating the mysteries of life and the universe."

"And beyond?"

"Nice try but the wrong movie."

They sat in quiet contemplation for several minutes until Simon said, "When the sky is clear like this and the stars are shining, it seems like I can almost see all the way to Heaven."

At this Fel began chuckling, a rare occurrence for her. Simon did not even know she could chuckle. The chuckling quickly turned into outright laughter. Fel's laugh was like that of a young child, which in many ways she was. Simon enjoyed listening to it, even as he suspected that he was the cause of it.

Four minutes later, after Fel had stopped laughing and had caught her breath, she said, "Oh but that felt good. After so many millennia of misery, it always feels good. Forgive me, Simon, but I could not help myself. What you said about Heaven?"

"What about it, Fel?"

"For all your knowledge you don't know, do you? None of you do. We are, all of us, already in Heaven. This world, this universe, all the worlds, all the universes, and what you call realities, are all part of the Divine. It was created from the Divine and so is a part of it. We are a part of it, and it is up to each of us to find our proper place."

Fel was quiet after that. Guessing her mood and what she might be thinking, Simon said softly, "You'll find your place as well."

"I had a part. I served the Word. Then a brief loss of faith, a moment of indecision, the wrong Choice and I was condemned. First an angel, then a demon, and now, I don't know. A mage's apprentice, serving a mortal when I once served the Divine. No offense intended."

"None taken, Fel."

"You won't beat me, will you?"

"Maybe later, and only if you ask nicely. But, Fel, I don't think it was chance that you were in a place to claim Felicia Baker's body. There is no chance or luck in the Pit. It is possible that you were meant to do so. As to why I don't know. But we will work toward finding your place, both here and hereafter. Now, for a few minutes more, let's look out upon infinity and beyond."

"And everything."

"That too."

But Simon's further contemplation of infinity was not to be. Nor did any spanking, punitive or otherwise take place, not in Simon's apartment anyway. The sound of sirens filled the night sky then the street below was filled with red and blue flashing lights, the vehicles that bore them stopping in front of the hotel.

"This is not good," Simon said, standing up and looking down.

"What's not good?"

"Fel, in this or any other sizable city you can tell how serious an incident is just by the number of emergency vehicles that arrive. I count two ambulances and four marked patrol cars. There are also two unmarked cars. That detectives have shown up this early tells me that this is not the first time whatever it is has happened. Of course, the aptly-named Starry Night is a boutique hotel, catering to guests willing to pay three to four times the average room rate for extreme personal service. So there's only one thing to do."

"What's that?"

"What do I always tell you to do when you don't understand something?"

"Google it."

"The other option."

"Ask somebody."

"So that's what I'm going to do. I'm going to ask somebody."

"Can I come with you?"

Simon looked at his companion. She was already dressed for bed, if "dressed" was the right word for it. Despite a slight chill in the air, Fel, was dressed only in sleep shorts and a thin cotton tank top. The top bore evidence of a chill in the air. As Simon was still in street clothes, he decided not to wait for her to change.

"You wait here. I'll let you know if I need any help."

"You won't have to. I'll know."

As he took the stairs to the street, Simon reflected, not for the first time, that maybe he was getting too close to this demon in a woman's body who had been placed in his charge. He was still debating if that was a good thing or a bad thing when he walked out on the street.

Standing on the sidewalk across from it, Simon watched the activity in front of the Starry Night. There was not much to see. Uniformed officers standing behind yellow barrier tape, warning off pedestrians, press, and angry guests who were temporarily barred from getting to their rooms.

Hopefully, they'll take refuge in Sebastian's, Simon thought as he watched the latter trying to decide what to do. *It is right across the street and business has been slow lately.* He wondered if it would be improper to cross the street and make that suggestion. He decided it was but was going to do so anyway when he saw paramedics wheel out two gurneys and load each into separate ambulances. As the ambulances sped off in the direction of Shock Trauma, Simon spied a familiar but probably not friendly face. He slowly crossed the street and stood close enough to the barrier tape for the officer to take notice of him but not to consider him as a threat to try and cross over.

"You'll have to move away, sir," the officer told him.

"I understand, Officer," Simon said stepping back, "but would you be so kind as to tell Detective Payne that Simon Tombs would like a word with him. Oh, never mind, he sees me now. Thank you, Officer Chambers, for all you do for the city."

Simon took a few more steps back and waited as the detective ducked under the yellow tape and walked up to him.

"Good evening, Timothy, or rather, evening, given the circumstances."

"It's 'Detective' to you, Tombs. And what are you doing here."

"My building is right across the street and when I saw all the commotion I came down to find out what was going on."

"Tombs, Sergeant Hood has given us instructions about talking to you."

"So Caitlin made sergeant, how nice for her. It must because she broke that serial killer case, the one nobody but she believed was a serial case." *The one I solved for her, although she did not come out of it unscarred.* "When you see her tell her I said congratulations. She won't return any of my calls. But I'm sorry, what did Caitlin say about talking to me?"

"She said not to. Now if you'll excuse me, Tombs."

"Just one minute, Detective Payne," Simon said in a way that commanded Payne's attention. Simon could have that effect on people, when he wanted to. "Don't think of me as Simon Tombs. Rather, think of me a concerned member of the community, one who has the mayor, the president of the city council, and the archbishop of Baltimore all on speed dial, by their first names, of course."

"You're bluffing, Tombs."

"Try me, Tim. You can tell me what's going on, why the full-scale assault? Or do I call Brandon and ask him. I'll try not to mention your name although I can't make any promises."

The expression on Payne's face was one of a man who's lost the game. "Okay, Tombs, but not here. And I'm only telling you as a concerned member of the community. You have to promise to keep out of it."

"Very well, Detective, you have my word. And I would sooner break my leg than break my word. Now may I suggest we go over to Sebastian's?" At Payne's hesitation, Simon added, "Consider it as part of the neighborhood canvas. The bartenders there are very observant."

"It was a robbery," Simon explained to Fel when he returned to their apartment after he and Detective Payne had parted company. Payne was very forthcoming with information, especially after trying one of Murphy's "Hotter Chocolates." Simon was not sure what Murph put into the drink but he was sure that most of it was something Payne should not have been drinking while on duty. Simon told Murph to make sure to put everything on his tab and to make sure Payne left after his second cup. A whispered spell made sure that the detective would suffer no effects other than a warm glow and a friendly feeling toward well-meaning mages.

"Of course the people who were robbed and beaten were tourists, rich ones at that. And they weren't the first. Detective Tim told me that the reason for the all-out response was that there has been a series of crimes against tourists and other revelers of the night who might appear to be easy targets. Three other hotel room invasions and four, possibly five street robberies. All the victims were savagely assaulted and most are still in the hospital. No one's dead yet but that's due mainly to the excellence of care one receives in Shock Trauma. Still, it's only a matter of time before someone is killed."

"Where are these crimes taking place, Master?"

Fel only called Simon "Master" on certain occasions. Her use in this instance meant that she was upset and taking this matter very seriously. He knew what she would expect him to do. But due to his given word he was going to have to disappoint her, maybe.

"All in this area, Fel. Within the few square blocks that surround us are bars, restaurants, theaters, theme taverns, and artfully disguised palaces of pleasure that the city knows about but pretends aren't there. People come here to have a good time, to relax and forget their worries for a night, or a weekend, or a week. And in relaxing and forgetting they let down their guard. Even the locals lose the basic caution that comes from living in an urban jungle."

Getting up from his spot on the couch, Simon again went out on the balcony. Fel followed and stood beside him. Looking down at the still present police cars, he said, "It hasn't hit the news yet, but it will. And when it does, tourism in Baltimore, especially in this area, will drop like a head from a guillotine. Many of the bright lights that you can see from here will go dark."

"What are we going to do about it?"

That was the question he had been expecting. "Nothing." At Fel's look of surprise, Simon said, "In order to get this information I had to give my word not to involve myself. And while I'm always willing to bend, break, or ignore rules and laws when I must or when I just feel like it, I will not break my word except under dire circumstances. And that," he pointed towards the Starry Night, "is not a dire circumstance."

Fel pulled away from him, disappointed in her master, mentor, friend, and lover. But she did not leave the balcony, did not take refuge in her room. Which Simon took as a good sign.

Wait for it, he thought. *See if she figures out on her own.*

"Simon?"

"Yes, Fel?"

"You said that you had given your word."

"Yes, I did."

"But I did not give mine."

"No, you did not. So what are you going to do about it?"

Fel went out the next evening. Wearing black and dark red, what she thought of as the colors of the night, she walked the streets of her neighborhood, searching for those who would harm others. She returned to Simon disappointed.

"Any luck?" he asked, already suspecting the answer.

"None. One would think there were no criminals out there,

that Baltimore is the safest place outside of the Holy Realm."

"What did you do? Walk and look around hoping to see crimes committed?" Simon could tell by her face that that was exactly what she had done.

Since Fel's "birth" in the body of Felicia Baker, Simon had taught her many things about life, love, humanity, and magic. It was time to teach the former denizen of Hell how to seek out evil intent.

"That's not the way these things work. It if was, the police would have a much easier time of it and would not require my ..." On seeing the look on her face he amended his statement, "... our occasional help. To find the bad guys you must track them down. Caitlin and her coworkers do so through investigation, using witness statements and evidence to identify their prey. I do it by various magics, some innate and others acquired at great cost. You know some simple magic but not enough, not for what you're trying to do."

"Then what do I do? There is something about these crimes that call to me to help stop them, but I don't know how to do it."

"Fel, this might be difficult for you, but within your human and oh so young and beautiful human body is an angelic nature." Before Fel could object Simon went on. "Yes, I said angelic. Even if They have stripped you of your wings and frisbeed away your halo, your essence was touched by the Divine and remains so. It has, however, been soiled and charred from your millennia in the Pit. How else were you able to dispatch the loathsome Weston Ellis so effectively?"

"I don't want to think about that, Simon. What I did, how I did it ..."

"Fel, my darling, daring demon, there is a darkness within all of us and none who are on the side of the Godly want to think about it. But it is there. Use that darkness as a weapon against those who rejoice in theirs. Like calls to like, that is the first lesson of magic. Actually, the first lesson is how to pull a rabbit out of a hat, but that trick never works. But use a small part of your dark nature to find the human demons here on Earth."

"And what if I find myself embracing the darkness within me?"

"Then I will say the words and send you back. But I do not think that will happen. I believe in you, Fel. If I did not you would not be sharing my work, my bed, and my life."

Fel didn't reply. Instead, she walked past Simon and out on to the balcony. She looked down at the street, then raised her head and looked between the tall buildings at Simon's starry bit of blackness. She stayed outside until a worried Simon joined her.

"Tomorrow night I will try. I will use the darkness within me to hunt those who would hurt others." She went to him and held him close. "But for tonight, I think you said something about sharing your bed?"

She went again the next evening. "Remember the rules, Fel," Simon had cautioned.

"Yes, *Master*," she replied in a sarcastic tone she had learned from him. "No killing and if possible, no witnesses."

"And the most important one?"

"Don't get caught."

"That's my girl."

Fel walked the streets of what she regarded as "her" neighborhood. As Simon had suggested, she looked inward and found the darkness inside her, the darkness that had developed then festered in her for several millennia. It had been all around her, reminding her of her sin, of her betrayal of the Three. She knew then what to search for. Pushing her own dark nature down into the recess of her soul, she opened herself to the darkness around her.

At first, it was almost too much. So many people out, all of them a mix of good and bad, of light and dark.

"Filter them out, Fel," Simon had told her. "Search not just for darkness but intent and desire. Those who want to do evil and are planning on it."

So Fel walked and waited, pushing aside those who would commit most of the seven deadly sins as long they did not plan to involve the unwilling, the unknowing, or the unconscious. Instead, she searched for one who planned to do evil that night.

The first was a would-be mugger. As she approached him she

felt him regard her as a possible victim. She slowed so that they would meet at an ungated areaway. He would push her in, then threaten to rob her. She would then alter his plan. But as she approached him he suddenly turned away, crossing the street before she got near.

She let him walk away, then followed at a distance. Although there was no need, she kept him in sight, the better to intervene when the time came. Several minutes and some blocks later, it did.

A young couple, teens perhaps on their first date. Like many who came to this part of Baltimore, they made the mistake of believing that bright lights and busy streets meant safety. The mugger followed them. Fel hurried after the mugger.

He came up behind the couple. Fel was close enough to hear, "Wallet, purse, phones, or she gets the knife."

She felt their fear, her worry, his desire to protect her warring with not wanting to get either of them injured. Before he could do something brave and stupid Fel was upon them. Grabbing the mugger from behind, she threw him against a wall. Her leg kicked out, his kneecap shattered. To the couple she said,

"You're safe. Go now, enjoy your evening and each other."

They ran one way, Fel walked the other. (Simon's advice. "Always walk, Fel, never run unless there's danger. People who run have something to hide and are likely to be chased.")

The mugger was found some minutes later, prompting the arrival of the paramedics and police. When they searched him, the responding officers found in his pockets cash, credit cards, and cell phones, none of which belonged to him.

Fel prevented other two robberies and one carjacking that night. From her encounter with the mugger, she knew what to look for and decided not to wait for them to choose a victim. Proactively she stalked those with ill intent, injuring two and convincing the third that it would be better to rent a car rather than steal one. All three encounters went quickly. No deaths, no permanent injuries, and as far as she knew, no witnesses.

Fel was on her way back to the apartment. She needed to see Simon. She needed to talk to him, she needed to do things that did not involve talking but rather sighs and guttural moans. A block away from her building she heard a cry for help.

She followed it into an alley. There she saw a man standing over a middle-aged woman. Her face was bloody and her clothing torn. The man was undoing his pants. Fel moved in.

It was quick, violent, and bloody. When it was over the man would not be capable of what he had intended to do for some time, if ever.

Finding the man's phone, Fel handed it to the woman. "Call for help," she said. "You did not see me."

The woman nodded her understanding. "Thank you," she said. "You're an angel."

Smiling, Fel said, "Close but not quite."

When she was back with Simon, he asked, "How did it go?"

"It went ... well."

"Righteous anger and justifiable mayhem?"

"Something like that?" She did not provide details. He did not ask for any.

"Simon, I need ..." She needed him. Excitement from a successful hunt, the thrill of knowing that she had done well and protected her own filled her full of passion and lust. But that need was outweighed by another.

"Yes?" Simon asked.

"I need ... to be alone."

Fel went out on the balcony and stared between the two buildings into the night sky. It was only when she looked down at the hotel between them that she was reminded that whatever good she had done, she had failed in her ultimate mission.

Somewhat humbled by this, she asked the night sky and Whoever might be watching her from behind it, "What am I? What was I and what will I become?"

"It's been three nights now and I am still no closer to finding the ones who attacked those people across the street," Fel told Simon over dinner.

"And if you go out tonight and tomorrow morning you will still be no closer. There has been talk that in order to calm this part of the city the BPD has launched an undercover task force that has little regard for procedures or suspects' rights. The police have denied this but of course they would."

"But if they are doing this then I am not nee… Oh, I am the task force."

"Yes, you are. And a very effective one at that. The word is out that someone is hunting the hunters. I expect to hear from Caitlin anytime now. I have my lies all prepared for when she calls. But you're right, the ones you set out to find are still out there."

"How do I find them?"

"Go to the source." Simon pointed out the window and toward the Starry Night Hotel. "It's been several days, but according to my new friend in the Crime Scene Unit, the one we saw at work in the abandoned school, every contact leaves a trace. So there will still be lingering traces of the evil committed there. Find and remember them."

"And then?"

"The hardest part of all. Wait. Do nothing. Let the area return to its normal rhythms. They will return. When they do you will sense them."

"And then I find and punish them."

"Something like that. In the meantime, do you remember the rules?"

"I remember, *Master*. No killing and if possible, no witnesses, and don't get caught."

"Fel, the souls I steal from the Pit, despite their sins, do they deserve redemption?"

"So you tell me."

"And creature of the Pit that you were, do you deserve redemption?"

"I'm trying to, Master."

"Something to consider, Fel."

Slowly, Simon's neighborhood returned to normal. Crime returned. That convinced most people that the media's speculation about a secret task force was true, since once the rumor went viral, the assaults, street robberies, and hold-ups began again.

Every night, Fel stood on the balcony and waited. That there were people below it whom she could have protected, should have been protecting, bothered her. She wondered, given her nature, why she should care about them. People called, Mama Fortuna for one, that woman Jillian for another. Simon left and came back. Fel stayed behind and waited.

She felt it a week after her last night out. It woke her up from a sound sleep. She left Simon's side and, being careful not to disturb the small boa constrictor that was sharing their bed, put on a robe and went out on the balcony.

As Simon had taught her, she opened her mind.

There were two of them, a man and a woman. A couple is safe. No one suspects them. They can go anywhere without question. Of course, it helps if they are attractive, well-dressed, and attentive to each other just to the point of unseemly open displays of affection.

They had stopped what they called their "fun and games" just before the task force rumors surfaced. They could afford to. They had taken enough money from their victims and had committed enough violence to satisfy themselves for a time. So they found a nice quiet Airbnb in Canton and, well, satisfied themselves until their carnal appetites waned and called out to be spiced up by the sufferings of others. By then the "task force" was commonly believed to have been disbanded although the local media, several social activists, and a few members of the City Council were loudly calling for a full investigation of the BPD's action in this matter, despite a complete absence of any evidence that the police were involved.

It was time to hunt again. Time to feel the mutual thrill that comes only with the infliction of pain on other human beings.

At first, the couple just drove around, looking for a place and an opportunity. It was when they drove by the Starry Night, unaware of the watcher on the balcony across the street, that they decided to begin where they had left off.

They were in the lobby when she came in – a medium sized brunette wearing new but not quite fashionable, off the rack clothing. She had a suitcase on wheels and another in her hand as she addressed the desk clerk loudly, her accent proclaiming her to be from someplace far south of Baltimore.

"Do you have any rooms? I got into the city late and the hotel down the street just gave away my room. I really need a place to stay, if only for tonight."

The look on the desk clerk's face said it all. *Why do they come when I'm on duty? Don't they know what kind of place this is? Even if we weren't fully booked months in advance this one could not afford our rates.*

That's what the desk clerk thought. But because of her last counseling session, and the hotel manager had made it clear that it was her *last* counseling session, what she said was,

"I'm very sorry, but we have no vacancies, but if you care to wait in the lobby I'll call around to see if I can find a place to accommodate you. Did you have a price range in mind?"

The Starry Night's daily rate was at least three times the average for Baltimore. Belying her appearance, the stranded tourist mentioned a rate that exceeded that, then offered, "And tell them I'm willing to pay cash."

"There is no torrent like Greed" the Buddha once said. It is not only one of the deadliest sins, it tends to make people stupid and careless. As the desk clerk made some calls and wondered how much of a "service fee" she could charge the woman, the couple waiting in the lobby talked quietly between themselves.

"She's perfect," he whispered.

"And has a nice shape hidden under those awful clothes," she replied. "Not that that matters."

It didn't. The couple long ago learned that forgoing sexual violence only heightened their own carnal experience later on. But it was so much fun to damage a beautiful body.

"How should we do this? The Good Samaritan?" he suggested

"Only works if we already have a room. We follow her then do Housekeeping."

"Agreed."

Standing up, he said loudly, "Let's go. I don't think they're going to show up." The couple left and waited outside for their prey.

Who left in a summoned taxi ten minutes later, after paying only a twenty dollar service fee. The hotel that had been found for her was a small one near BPD headquarters. When the woman got out of her cab, the couple was right behind her. They checked in one after the other, the couple hearing to what room the woman had been assigned.

As the three people went up in the same elevator they were watched by a man in the lobby. He was a tall man with blue-gray eyes. If he had permitted anyone to take notice of him they would have said he was handsome and might have observed that his features indicated that had seen just about everything and done most of it.

Simon had thought to intercept the couple, to ask them if they would not reconsider their actions, to offer them the Choice. But he had promised not to interfere, and so he left them to whatever fate and Fel had in store.

The couple checked in. They would wait until their target was settled before they struck. Fel did not wait.

"Housekeeping." Her knock on the room door was answered. She barged in and did what she had to do.

When the couple judged that enough time had passed, they went to the woman's room. The door opened before they had the chance to knock. Strong hands grabbed their wrists and dragged them inside. They were then thrown across the room and on to the farthest bed.

Like Simon in the lobby of this hotel, no one had noticed Fel in the lobby of the Starry Night. Not being noticed was part of the magic Simon had taught her. On learning to what hotel the woman had been directed, she left ahead of the taxi's arrival and was waiting along with Simon in the lobby. Still unnoticed by the three people, she got on the same elevator as they did and followed the woman to her room. Only then did she wait. And as she waited, she thought and considered.

The couple recovered. They stood and wondered what had happened to the brunette. Their wondering did not stop them from drawing weapons – her a pistol, him a knife – and coming toward Fel. She disarmed them, none too gently. She then again threw one by one across the room, this time past the farthest bed and dangerously close to the window.

This time the couple stood but, cradling their shattered wrists, they stayed where they were. "Who the hell are you?" the man asked.

It was the same question Fel had been asking herself. It was only now that she knew the answer.

"I am this neighborhood's guardian … demon," Fel answered, ignoring the pounding on the inside of the bathroom door. "And for what you two have done, you deserve to seek your answers in the place you named. But after much consideration, I have decided that it not for me to send you there. The Choice is yours."

So you're letting us go?" the woman asked with hopeful surprise.

"I did not say that," Fel said as she slowly walked toward the couple.

A phone call from a throwaway cell led police to the hotel not far from their headquarters. A frightened but otherwise unharmed woman was rescued from a bathroom from which the inner knob of its door had been removed. Paramedics were called for the severely injured couple found sprawled across the furthest bed. DNA tests would later show that all the blood in the room was theirs. The DNA and their fingerprints would also prove to be a match to the series of robberies that Detective Timothy Payne had told Simon about. How they got into the room, and how they came to be in that state was a mystery to all but two detectives.

They met at Zeke's on Harford Road, far away from their curious co-workers and any possible listening devices rumored to have been installed by Inspectional Services.

"Payne, what exactly did Tombs say when you told him what was going on at the Starry Night?"

"I already told you, Sarge."

"Tell me again," Caitlin Hood ordered. "His exact words."

Although Timothy Payne had been under the influence of two

cups of Hotter Chocolate, he still remembered what Simon Tomb had said to him. "He said, 'You have my word, Detective, I will not interfere in this investigation'. Now I know you don't like the guy much, Sarge, neither do I, he's a pain in the ass, but as far as I know, he never breaks his word."

"I know but still …" Then it occurred to Caitlin. A pretty young blond wearing almost nothing at all, openly flirting with her, Tombs not seeming to care. Caitlin had dreamed about her, dreams that later turned to a nightmare of that blonde's arm going through a man's chest. She could have done it. She had done it. And she had not been covered by Tombs's word.

"What wrong, Sarge? It's Tombs, isn't it? What are we going to do about him?"

"Nothing, Payne. There's nothing we can do except close this case and take what credit's to be had. But the next time, let Tombs make the damn phone call."

Only Mostly Dead

There is a certain shop in every city where people like Simon Tombs live. It has no name, but those who need to can find it. If they cannot they will not long survive the dangerous game they dare to play. Those who work in the shop do not ask their patrons' names, nor do they offer their own. It is of necessity a cash or barter business.

In Baltimore, the shop (Simon always thought of it as The Shoppe) appeared to be a vacant store across from an elementary store on Old Harford Road. Battered signage declared it to have once been a church and then a comic book store. In the morning and mid-afternoon, the parking lot was used by parents dropping off or picking up their children.

No one saw Simon enter. Nor would anyone see him leave. It was part of the glamour of The Shoppe.

The usual pleasantries were exchanged. Remarks about the weather, comments on the latest game, opinions about current events. That the events were not current but may have happened years ago or not at all, that the sports teams belonged to a league that had never played in Baltimore, or that the climate remarked upon did not match the weather outside did not bother Simon. He was used to it. He was also used to the fact that the person (if person it was) behind the counter always knew exactly what he wanted.

He was handed a package. "Not easy to come by," the salesperson said. "Freely given and all that. Plus the source. Fewer and every year. Or so it seems."

Simon agreed and paid what was asked – in cash. Barter was always much too risky. He left with a lighter wallet but an easy mind.

It was best to be prepared when one was in a ghost story.

It all started when Simon received a phone call from his favorite bookseller.

"Ginny, to what do I owe the pleasure?"

"If it's pleasure you want, young man, stop at the store after closing. There'll be forty-five years of experience waiting for you."

Simon, who could have matched then exceeded Virginia London in life experiences, smiled to himself then replied. "Ginny, I doubt if I would survive the encounter."

"But what a way to go, ey, love? Or it is that you're too busy with *her*?"

"*Her*" was Simon's companion. "Don't worry about Fel, Ginny. I can handle her."

"I'm sure you've done your fair share of handling. It's you I'm worried about. I want to make sure you haven't bit off more than you can swallow. Or is she doing most of the swallowing?"

Memories of another time, another life, another name came to the fore. Again Simon smiled as he pushed them back done. "What can I do for you, Ginny?"

He knew she hadn't called for casual conversation. She never did. Back in the day, she never had. So it had to be something important, to her or to him.

"A young lady named Katrina Powers came into the store earlier today. She said that she read on the internet that London's Books was known for its esoteric and occult selections. And that needing an expert in those matters she drove to Baltimore to see me."

"Ginny, my dear, did you tell her that you placed that article yourself?'

"Bait for new agers and hipsters, Simon. These days an independent bookseller has to use every trick. Anyway, when she told me what her problem was I thought of you."

"What is her problem and how far did she come?"

"She said she was from Ocean City, and that the place she works for might be haunted."

"Did she happen to mention where she worked?" Simon asked, beginning to get the feeling that things were about to spiral out of control and that he should start looking for a soft place to land.

"Some fancy hotel called the Gold Castle."

Better known as *Le Chateau D'Or.* The spiraling became more certain and Simon reflected that however soft it might appear, hitting the sand from a height of twelve stories was not anywhere close to a soft landing.

"So I told her that I would call you and if you were interested you would meet her tonight at six at Fortuna's. And that's my good deed for the day. Stop by the store sometime, Simon, I've got some more of those Murphy books you like so much."

As usual, Ginny hung up without saying goodbye, leaving Simon to think about things going around and coming around, and however much he wanted to skip dinner at Fortuna's he knew he didn't dare. And how little time he had to properly prepare.

Fortuna's was a restaurant in Baltimore's historic Fells Point. It was located just off Broadway near the market and if you didn't know it was there you'd walk right by it. There was gambling on the second floor and activities best not talked about in the basement. But Simon was not there for either of those.

As she usually did when he came to dine, Momma Fortuna greeted Simon personally and led him to the best table.

"*She* is not with you tonight?"

Simon did not need to ask about whom Momma was asking. Nor did he miss the tone of concern and slight disapproval in her voice.

"You've heard then."

"Most of us have, although the story of how you acquired her and for what reasons vary. Shouldn't she be here, at your side?"

In other words, Simon thought, *why have I let a creature from the Pit out of my sight?*

"Nothing to worry about, Momma. Right now she's in my apartment watching a triple feature of Rosemary's Baby, the Exorcist, and The Omen."

"Should she be watching them?"

"She thinks they're comedies. Besides, I'm meeting someone here. Someone with a problem, one I think it best that my new ...

companion … not be involved with."

Momma nodded and gave Simon a look that only an old friend and one-time lover could give. Then she turned him over to a waiter who brought him a glass of the house wine and an appetizer of fries covered in gravy.

By the time Katrina Powers was shown to his table, the fries were gone and Simon was on his second glass of wine.

"Mr. Tombs, I'm so sorry I'm late. Are traffic and parking always this bad in this area. This part of town is safe, isn't it? I mean, I've heard stories and …"

Feeling that unless he interrupted the woman sitting across from him would chatter herself into a panic, Simon said, "Ms. Powers, relax." He signaled his waiter, who brought another glass of Momma's excellent wine. "Take a breath, have a sip of wine, then take another drink. To save time I've already ordered, a surf and turf platter for two. We will eat, we will drink, and then over dessert you can tell me why you think your house is haunted."

When what had been the best cheesecake she had ever eaten was halfway done, Katrina said, "It's not really a house. It's a condominium east of the city."

Simon held up his hand. "Ms. Powers, my favorite bookseller told me that you were from Ocean City, that *Le Chateau d'Or* had a ghost problem, and asked if I could help. Since there is almost nothing I won't do for Ginny London, not excepting the odd misdemeanor and an occasional felony, I agreed. However, now since our waiter is giving us an impatient but always correct and polite stare, I suggest we pay the bill, leave a generous tip, and open up our table to whoever is next in line. I know the perfect place to discuss ghoulies, ghosties, and ill-mannered beasties."

The perfect place was the observation deck of Baltimore's World Trade Building. That it was after hours did not stop Simon. He entered with a key and was ignored by the night guard. Minutes later he and Katrina were looking out over Baltimore's Inner Harbor while she started her ghost story.

Not wishing to confirm his growing suspicion that he was probably the root cause of the haunting, Simon asked,

"Is it just one apartment you believe to be haunted or the entire building?'

"I don't know if the whole building is affected but certainly several of the units."

Damn, Simon thought. "What makes you suspect the supernatural rather than a more mundane explanation – noisy pipes, the ground settling, human error and wrongdoing?'

"Well, a few months ago there was a murder."

Double damn. "I didn't hear of any murders in Ocean City. Killings there are usually big news here in Baltimore. They tend to distract people from the local ones."

"You wouldn't have heard about this one. The management of *Le Chateau D'Or* made sure of it."

Simon knew of the murder which Katrina Powers had mentioned. He was the one who had pulled the trigger. Nor had that been the only killing that night, a night that led to a little girl being rescued and the "birth" of his semi-reformed demonic companion Fel.

Not wishing to confess to crimes of which he was not suspected, Simon said, "Murders happened all the time, even in exclusive condominiums. They don't usually result in hauntings. What else? Are the residents complaining of rattling chains, dread specters, or moanings at night not caused by passion?"

"The sound-proofing in the units is very good, the best. Any moaning, for any cause, would not be heard outside them."

Nor would a gunshot, Simon thought. *I wonder how long before the body was found.* Katrina continued.

"No strange noises and all the blood on the walls has been accounted for. Some of the residents, however, have reported seeing … things … in the hallways."

"How many residents? What kind of things?"

Katrina hesitated before answering, as if she didn't want to believe in spooks but, like the Cowardly Lion, had no choice but to do so.

"Several. More than five, less than ten. Some of the reports are hearsay. Someone told him and he told me kinds of reports. And the things they've seen range from a cloud of vapor to a 'man-sized object that passed through the wall of the third-floor lobby.'"

Simon looked out over the harbor. He could remember when it was a working port, receiving and shipping goods. He was someone else then, and the harbor something else – dirty and warehouse filled, the water polluted to the point it would sometimes catch fire. Baltimore back then was a place to drive through, not to, it's only attraction being the red-light zone known as the Block.

Now people take their vacations there. The National Aquarium, the Maryland Science Center, the Ravens and the Orioles. Every spring and summer weekend there seems to be another event, although Simon wished they'd move the Baltimore Book Festival back to Mount Vernon.

Simon looked past this, past the Domino Sugar sign. He thought about Fort McHenry, and how its five-sided design had protected the city from more than just the British. What would people think if they knew that the battle that gave the USA its national anthem wasn't a battle at all but a joint effort to drive out an ancient evil?

"Mr. Tombs? Are you okay?"

Simon broke from his reverie. "Sorry, Ms. Powers, lost in thought. You just might have a ghost. Have there been break-ins?"

"Yes, how did you know?"

If the building was haunted it was a logical development. To Katrina he merely shrugged and said, "It's what I do. Now let me guess. No signs of forced entry. Nothing showing on what I suppose is the best surveillance system money can buy?"

"Better, Mr. Tombs, money can't buy what we use. And no, not even a vaporous cloud. The odd thing is that nothing was taken in any of the break-ins. The only reason anyone knew their apartment had been entered is that …"

"Things in them had been moved." At Katrina's nod Simon said, "Mr. Powers, there is a very good chance that *Le Chateau D'Or* has at least one ghost, possibly more than one."

"A good chance? What else could it be?"

Simon smiled. "An undigested bit of beef, a blot of mustard, a fragment of an underdone potato. Let me tell you a story. There is a house right here in Baltimore that was said to be haunted. If we were to turn away from the harbor and look northward over the city I could point out its general location. The owner died in an arson fire and the neighbors swore that whenever the full moon rose his ghost could be seen in the room where he died."

"And could it?"

Simon shook his head. "The ghost was nothing more than the reflection of the moon in a window whose glass was slightly warped by the fire."

"And what did the neighbors say when you told them the truth?"

"Who said I told them? The ghost made their neighbor special so why let the truth get in the way of a good story? Now, if I am to go ghost hunting I need to make preparations. Why don't we plan on my meeting you down the ocean tomorrow evening?"

Katerina looked disappointed. "I didn't really come prepared to stay over in Baltimore. I don't have anything to sleep in. For that matter, anywhere to sleep. I was hoping we could drive down tonight. Unless you can recommend a good place to sleep over?"

The invitation was obvious. But Simon had learned long ago not to mix work and play. Besides, there was Fel to consider. She would be mad enough by his leaving her alone for what might be several days.

"Why not? Fools rush in where demons fear to tread." *And maybe you'll tell me everything you've left out tonight.*

"I thought that was angels."

"Not in my world." *Angels are fearless*, Simon thought. At least the few he'd met.

A quick trip home to gather his things. A brief argument with Fel about why he couldn't bring her along. A warning for her to stay out of trouble, and if she couldn't not to get caught. He then left for Sebastian's, which is where he had arranged to meet Katrina.

While he waited for Katrina Simon sipped a Pepper Special and thought about the last ghost story in which he was involved.

A house in Baltimore County. The original owners fleeing in

the middle of the night for parts unknown. After the house was seized and sold for unpaid back taxes, the new owners complained of unexplained noises, occasional odd odors, a general feeling of uneasiness, and the fact that even in the summer the house always seemed cold.

Simon was called in when the apparition appeared. A young girl, still mostly a child, holding a child of her own. He took the chance of entering her world and speaking to her. He learned of her life, and her death, and her baby. He discovered that her older brother was responsible for the latter, and her father for other two.

Simon tracked down the family. What he did then was violent, messy, and highly illegal. It cost him a small part of his soul but did bring peace to the girl and her child. The baby moved on but the girl remains a ghost, a protective spirit watching over the family that now lives in her house.

Somehow I don't this will work out as well, Simon was thinking as Katrina pulled up in front.

"I forgot to ask last night," Simon said as Katrina pulled off I-895 and onto 97, "what exactly is it you do at *Le Chateau D'Or?*"

"I work for building management."

A properly evasive answer, he thought. *Let's see if she can do better.*

"And how many deaths have occurred since the murder?"

"Just the on … you know, don't you?"

Simon didn't, but he had guessed. A condominium is more like a house than an apartment. Someone owns it. A ghost, even one like Magister Collin Reynolds, if that who the spirit was, would likely have been confined to one area, or one floor. From what Katrina had told *Le Chateau D'Or* was infested. More than one ghost resided there, and the greater number of spirits, the more the haunt will spread.

There was another possibility, one Simon thought likely given the circumstances. Which is why he had armed himself at The Shoppe with a relic of St. Andrew Avellino, medallions of the living and the dead, and a spirit knife. And he had one other knife that he had picked up the last time he was in Ocean City.

To Katrina he said, "Of course I know. What do you think I did between the time Ginny called and I met you at Fortuna's? Your employer may have covered things up but I make a habit of uncovering things. Now, tell me about the deaths."

Pretended knowledge is sometimes better than the real thing, and a good bluff can win the pot even when one is faced with aces full of kings.

"There were four – three suicides and a suspicious drug overdose. The family of the hanged man was led to believe that he had died from auto-erotic asphyxiation. They were more than willing to keep things quiet to avoid embarrassment. Likewise the family of the man who shot himself. They were Catholic and wanted to bury him in holy ground. The drug overdose was no problem. People on vacation experiment and sometimes tragedy results."

"And the last?"

"She slit her wrists in the bathtub. That's when we began to suspect we had a problem. All those crank complaints about clouds and shapes and burglaries that weren't all came together."

"And that's when you typed 'ghostbusters' into your search engine and hit enter."

"Something like that."

More likely, you knew or suspected of my connection with Ginny and used her to get to me. "What happened to her, the woman who slashed her wrists?"

"I don't know. The last I saw of her she was naked and bled out in her bathtub. The next day she was gone."

As they crossed the Chesapeake Bay Bridge Simon was both wishing he had never met Ms. Katrina Powers and glad that Ginny had called him. This was more than a ghost story. There was evil about, and deeper waters than the ones they were passing over.

Two hours later Simon was disappointed when Katrina pulled onto Route 90 and entered Ocean City over the Assawoman Bay Bridge. He preferred to stay on Route 50 and use the Harry W. Kelly Memorial Bridge, named after the late and legendary mayor of the ocean resort. The bridge took one into old Ocean City, past the guest houses and smaller hotels that were the city's mainstay before everyone caught condo fever.

But I'm not the one driving, he reflected as Katrina turned left off 90. Soon they were pulling into the VIP parking area of *Le Chateau D'Or*. Having left Baltimore around nine, it was now close to midnight.

"It's late," Katrina said. "I suppose you'll want to rest up and start fresh in the morning. We don't have any guest rooms, but one of the perks of my job is a small apartment."

One bed, no doubt, Simon thought, a little more tempted than he was in Baltimore. Katrina Powers was an attractive lady and he had made no promise of fidelity to Fel. Still, while Katrina may have been telling him the full and unvarnished truth it was just a likely that this was all an elaborate trap. After all, he had already encountered one former member of the Greater Key. There had to be a few more about.

"While I appreciate the offer, Ms. Powers, I prefer to get right to work. Midnight is almost upon us, the time when one day flows into the next. I'd like to take advantage of that."

This wasn't quite true. "Midnight" was an artificial concept, an arbitrary time set by man. Day into Evening, Night into Dawn, these were the magical times when Light and Darkness merged and gave way and anything was possible.

But just then midnight was a useful fiction, allowing Simon to put off Katrina's carnal invitation but not refuse her outright.

Simon's excellent hearing heard Katrina's *sotto voce* "At least you're taking advantage of something." As he was trying to decide if she had meant for him to hear that she said, "I suppose you'll want to start on the twelfth floor?"

And so the game begins, Simon thought. "Why, what's on the twelfth floor," he asked. If he hadn't, if he had simply agreed that was where he wanted to start, it would have been an indication that he knew more than she had so far revealed. As it was, it told Simon that his involvement in Magister Reynold's death was suspected if not known. That this was more than a ghost story was now evident. Simon could now smell the cheese of a trap baited just for him, and that added spice to this adventure.

"That's where the murder occurred."

"Oh, I see. I will definitely visit there, but first, if it will not disturb the residents who still believe their home by the shore to be spirit free, I would like to sit quietly in the lobby and, shall we say, take in the atmosphere. It will help in my locating the ghosts and identifying their natures. If you leave me your cell number, I'll call you when I need you again."

Katrina had tried and mostly succeeded in disguising her disappointment that she had failed to trip Simon up with her "twelfth-floor" question. She was less successful in hiding her pique at being summarily dismissed. Without a word she quickly wrote down her number and handed it to him. Smiling a "thank you," Simon found a chair, sat in it, and closed his eyes. Katrina waited until she realized she was being ignored, then left to do whatever it was building management did when they weren't trying to ensnare mages.

Simon considered building his mental bridge to the Pit and drawing strength from a repentant soul. He rejected that idea as soon as he thought of it. He didn't need that kind of power and it might be exactly what Katrina Powers was hoping he would do. He didn't know with whom she had made what kind of bargain.

The last time he was in Ocean City he had followed the song of a child's soul in order to find her. There were too many souls in *Le Chateau D'Or* that night – some asleep, some in bed but not alone and not sleeping. Others were no doubt sitting on their balcony wondering if the view and the exclusivity were worth what they had paid for them. So many souls, each with their own song.

Simon reviewed his protections. The relic of St. Andrew would protect him from the dead, the medallion of the dead would allow him to speak to them, while the medallion of the living would protect his mortal self as he did what he needed to do. As for the two knives, each had their own purpose.

Simon sent his consciousness out of his body and through the building, searching for lost souls. He found the first in a third-floor apartment. Other than the spirit of the hanged man the apartment was vacant. The shade was moving small objects from one place to another in a desperate attempt to be noticed. Simon sensed that this was the reason for his suicide, the need to be noticed, if only by someone who merely wondered why he would take his own life.

Simon almost moved on to searching for another who had given up on life and now was unable to find true death. But then he noticed a thin thread leading upwards from the spirit. It went through the ceiling and the mage suspected that it terminated on the twelfth floor. He studied, felt and learned its essence, and began to search for others like it.

The seventh floor, where a man whose back skull had been blown out by a large caliber weapon walked the halls, seeking a way out the building. A balcony on the eighth floor, when a forever teenaged boy coasted on his last high, with no need or desire to go any further. And in the bathroom of a tenth-floor apartment, the ghost of a woman desperately tried to staunch the flow of blood from her veins, regretting her actions yet unable to take them back. Her death was repeated over and over, even as a family of four used the bathroom as they got ready for bed.

All were linked, tied to each other by a ghostly thread which led upwards. Simon wondered what might happen if he used his spirit knife to cut the thread. Would they fade away to their final rewards or damnations, or was the thread the only thing keeping them from becoming more manifest?

Only one way to find out. The twelfth floor it was, where this began and would hopefully end.

Simon Tombs did not often make a mistake, although there were many who thought that Fel might prove to be his biggest one. When he did make one, he was usually the first to admit it.

Stepping off the elevator into the twelfth-floor apartment Simon realized that not only had he made a very bad mistake, it might just be his last.

When he was last in the apartment, that time months ago when he was looking for a missing child, its occupant, Magister Reynolds, had thought to trap him with a precast spell that prevented Simon from using his magic. As Reynolds was gloating over what he believed to be a coup Simon produced a pistol and shot him. With the magister dead, the spell should have faded.

I really should have made sure, Simon thought, as he saw the preserved body of the magister still on the living room floor where it had fallen. He felt the binding wrap around him. The spells he had prepared, the magic he had inside of him were useless to him now. And this time Simon had not brought his gun.

He heard Katrina before he saw her emerge from a rear bedroom. When she did he saw that she had not forgotten her gun and was pointing it at him.

"As you well know, Mr. Tombs, there's a big difference between mostly dead and all dead. The Magister is mostly dead. We reached him just seconds before life passed from his body and so were able to keep him alive."

"Pity," Simon replied. As his binding did not inhibit movement Simon was able to turn ad face Katrina, "I was hoping to go through his pockets for loose change." Looking back at the near lifeless body on the floor he added, "Why did you bother saving him? He doesn't seem to be of much use to anyone."

"He's not, Mr. Tombs. But it keeps him out of the Pit. Thanks to your interference he, along with the rest of us, have failed its masters and on death we must pay the price."

"Let me guess. You used what magic that was still in his body to 'encourage' feelings of despair, depression, and possibly boredom with life among the residents here. When they died you interrupted their journeys and used their souls as life support for …" Again he looked at Reynolds's body. "…that. I suppose the overdose was a nice surprise, unless you encouraged that as well.

"You went through a lot of trouble to bring me here. Why?"

"You have something of ours, Mr. Tombs. Something we need to complete the sacrifice you interrupted and so placate our Masters."

Been there, done that, released the demon, and now she works for me, Simon thought, then he started wondering what it was they needed.

The knife they were going to use in the ritual. Right now it's strapped to my right leg. But why, it's just an ordinary knife …

"Oh no, you can't mean …" he said out loud.

"But I do, Mr. Tombs. I don't know why you decided to spare Felicia Baker's life, or why you took her with you, or what you're doing with her. No, I can imagine what you're doing with her, or rather, to her. I can't imagine she's a willing captive."

They don't know. This could be fun, if I'm alive to enjoy it. "So you brought me all the way to Ocean City on the off chance I'd bring Fel, eh, Felicia with me."

"That would have been nice, but no, knowing that you would not able to resist a ghost story, particularly one that took place at the scene of one of your many crimes, we brought you here to get you out of the way. No sooner had we left Baltimore, several of our members began tracking Felicia to wherever you had her prisoner. By now she's been rescued and is on her way to the ritual site. There the sacrifice will be completed and one of our Masters will be released from the Deep Pit."

Simon did his best to surpass a laugh, He almost succeeded. "You don't know what you're doing."

"I think we do, Mr. Tombs."

"No, you really don't. But what now? You pull that trigger and use my soul to power that thing on the rug."

"Don't tempt me. No, it's been decided that you're to be offered to the master on his release from the Pit. I'm sure he will enjoy devouring you slowly."

Many years ago, in the time between the world wars, Simon had met a man after whom he patterned his current life. One thing this man had taught him was to always have an ace up one's sleeve. Preferably an ace with a sharp edge and a good throwing balance. That night Simon's ace was the spirit knife. He had meant to use it to sever the connection between the ghosts and this plane of existence. But needs must.

Holding his arm just so, Simon let the knife drop into his hand. Then in a move he had practiced over and over again until he could do it in his sleep (and once had) he sent the blade flying toward Katrina Powers while at the same time dropping to the floor and rolling behind a couch that he was sure would not be able to stop a bullet.

Katrina would have done better to have copied Simon and stopped, dropped, and rolled. Instead, she got off one shot, the bullet striking and digging into the carpet just as the knife found her left eye. She collapsed on the floor.

This time I make sure, Simon decided, *both of them*.

Pulling his second knife from the sheath under his pants leg, he approached what was left of Katrina Powers.

Something got to her first.

Even in his bound state, his magic in a state of suspension, Simon could see the tendrils reach for her, tendrils that connected her to the remains of Magister Reynolds. Slowly her body withered while at the same time Reynolds's grew healthier. Soon Katrina was a dried out husk. Reynolds on the other hand …

"Stupid bitch. I never did like her," he said, as he sat up, the bullet wound in his head closing up. Simon half expected him to spit the bullet into his hand and was disappointed when he didn't. Reynolds didn't look like the kind of man who would fall for the same trick twice. Still, Simon readied his knife.

"You'll not need that, Tombs," the magister said. Suddenly Simon felt the binding restricting his magic loosen and fade away. To his questioning look Reynolds replied, "I've just spent several months on the edge of death, at the brink of damnation, staring into the Abyss while it stared back and showed me what punishments awaited me and my kind. The Fallen don't care for us. Don't care what sins we commit for them. There is no reward in that place of eternal pain."

"So what are your plans?" Simon asked, keeping his knife at the ready while judging the distance between himself and Katrina's pistol.

"To use what time I have left to seek redemption. That is, if you'll permit me to leave."

"Alone and as you are, after you release those spirits bound to you."

"I didn't ask for that. But now I'm glad." Reynolds paused,

then "There, they're free. Free to face whatever Fate awaits them. And may the ... Three-in-One have mercy on their souls and count whatever they suffered at our hands as time served."

"That's a start, Reynolds. You can continue by stopping the sacrifice your followers ... ex-followers have planned."

Reynolds shook his head. "Too late for that. That drama will play out before either of us could do anything. You were right, they know not what they've done." He paused again, then "Let's see, I have a few hundred in my wallet, credit cards that may or not be good, and a decent bank account as long as that bitch," he gestured toward what was left of Katrina, "didn't drain it. There's a safe somewhere in this apartment, Tombs. Find it, open it, and use whatever is in there to do some good. And now if you'll excuse me, as the man said in the song, 'I have a long way to go and a short time to get there'. So I might as well get started."

With that Collin Reynolds walked out of his luxury apartment, down twelve flights of stairs, and into the night, seeking his salvation.

After flushing away the remains of Katrina Powers, he looked out the apartment window, past Old Ocean City, and toward Assateague Island, where a drama over which he had no control might be taking place.

She might not have let them take her, he thought. *Right now she could be trying to explain the presence of several dead bodies to Caitlin Hood. Or ...* Simon stopped thinking. He'd make his plans when he found Fel. Or she found him. In the meantime, there was a safe to locate and good deeds to plan with its contents.

Buried Memories

They waited until they saw Katrina Powers's car take the ramp for the Harbor Tunnel Thruway before driving into Baltimore and parking near Sebastian's, a bar the thief was known to frequent. They weren't looking for him, he was in the car with Katrina. No, they were looking for the woman he had stolen. He had interrupted their ritual, killed their Mistress, destroyed the child, and stolen the sacrifice.

She was somewhere close but they did not know where. The thief's home was shielded against them, they could sense no trace of her. But she was alone, and at night she would come out. There were rumors that someone prowled the nearby streets, hunting those who would hunt others. Katrina believed it was she, controlled by the thief, doing his bidding, gathering souls to feed his own.

They went into the bar and ordered drinks. Maybe they'd get lucky, maybe she would come in.

"She's been here, so has he," whispered Lucia Coffey, the sensitive of the group. She had become a Follower of the Golden Key the same time their quarry had, had known her intimately and carnally. "Magic has been done here, more than once. This is one of *his* places."

The others looked around as if the thief might suddenly appear. But there was no danger of that. He and Katrina, their new Mistress, were driving east on Route 50 towards Ocean City, towards a trap he thought was a ghost hunt.

"Any trace of her," asked Moses Hewitt, the group's leader.

Lucia shook her head. She closed her eyes, mentally searching for her one-time friend. "Not yet, no wait, it's her, yet not her. He's done something to her, to her mind. Grayed it out, fogged it so she'll do his bidding. When we find her I'll know for sure."

"Where is she?"

Jamal Livingston had asked this a little too loudly, drawing stares from the other patrons. The group looked at him but said nothing. They could remember when they were new to the Greater Key, excited by the sex, the power, and the promise of eternal freedom to do what one wilt.

"Close," Lucia said, "but moving away."

"Then we better move," Moses said. "Donald, bring the van around. Lucia, go with him. Tell him which way he'll have to go. We'll settle up here."

In five minutes they were gone, heading east in pursuit of she who had once been theirs.

The bartender and server watched them leave.

"What do you think, Amy?" the server asked. "Friends of Simon?"

"They're something, Murph, but I don't think they're his friends. They might be looking for him."

"Poor bastards."

"Or worse, that scary girlfriend of his."

"In that case, poor damned bastards."

The mostly reformed demon Fel was taking her nightly walk, "her patrol" Simon called it. Crime in the neighborhood had dropped to almost nonexistent since she started doing so, as if the other predators sensed that they were now prey to a more dangerous hunter. There were other people out walking as well; coming home from an evening out, breathing in the night air, and enjoying the freedom of being outside in city which had trapped them indoors for too long.

She was turning a corner to go down a darkened street, as if daring a would-be robber to mistake her for a potential target. He would survive, but would carry a painful reminder of the encounter for the rest of his days.

A Honda Odyssey pulled up alongside her, then cut her off as she was about to cross a side street. Fel smiled to herself. It had been a while. She just had to be sure to follow Simon's instructions and not get caught.

The van's driver's rear door slid open. A man and woman got.

Fel sensed two more behind her. *This is going to be fun*, she thought. *Simon should go away more often.*

"Felicia, it's us," the man in front said.

There was a part of her mind that was still Felicia Baker, the woman whom Simon had killed and thus opened for her a doorway from the Pit. From this part, she called up the names of the pair she was facing – Moses Hewitt and Elva Stone. She risked a quick glance, she didn't know the two behind her. The driver she did know, Donald Bartlett. When her body had been Felicia's she had been with them all, in every way possible.

Fel half turned, her back to the wall so she could keep them all in view. A mental intrusion from the woman she didn't know. Fel allowed her in, then, as Simon had taught her, blocked her and sent migraine-level pain back her way. The woman staggered but did not fall.

"Are you okay, Lucia," asked the young man beside her.

"I'm fine, Jamal. She's warded that's all."

A BPD patrol car drove slowly down the street, its lights shining on the five people on the sidewalk. As it seemed they were just talking, the marked unit moved on. There was a mutual release of breath as Fel asked,

"Moses, Elva, what do you want."

"We want you, Felicia. We've come to redeem you from the thief and return you to the ritual ground where you can complete your destiny."

"And if I don't want to go?"

Moses moved in closer, signaling Elva and Jamal to do the same. Donald got out of the van and stood by in case he was needed.

"A willing sacrifice is more welcome, but the masters of the Pit will always accept one is who is unwilling. A debt is owed. It's you unless you know where the child is."

No one knew that, Fel thought. Using his contacts Simon had hidden the girl, her father, and her adoptive mother so deep even he couldn't find them. They were different people living a different story, one far away from magic, demons, and devils.

Fel shook her head. "The child is gone, Si... my captor destroyed her." Close enough to the truth.

"Then it's you, or it's damnation for all of us."

"Isn't that where we're all headed, to Perdition when this life is over."

"Oh, Felicia, what did he do to you?" Elva asked. "By your sacrifice, that of the thief, and the others to follow, we will earn favor, favor for when we descend to our reward. We will be lords in Hell and not slaves, administering the punishments rather than receiving them."

Fel would have laughed had she not sensed that these five were true believers. Had it not been for the patrol car that had recently passed, and the fact that Simon might be captive (although she mostly doubted the latter) she would have sent them to their "reward" right then.

So she shrugged, as if in resignation. "What must be, must be," she said, echoing the words of a song Simon sometimes sang. He claimed to have known the singer in another life, when he had a different name. He told many such stories, she believed some of them.

"If you wish me to accompany you I will."

"Get in the van, Felicia," Moses ordered. None of the others said otherwise.

Fel had done what she had to do. She had delivered the warning, had offered them the Choice. That they did not recognize what had happened was not on her. There would be consequences, there would be a price. How steep of one she could not say.

The van left the city and traveled the same route that Simon and Katrina had taken. Fel sat in the third row, between Jamal and Elva. When the young man put his hand on her thigh and began to move it upwards she asked, "Which finger do you wish broken?"

Jamal's hand stopped but he did not remove it from her leg. "I belong to the one to whom I was promised," she told him. "The thief did not touch me for this reason," she lied. "I see no reason to allow you to do so."

"Keep your hands to yourself, Jamal, and your dick in your pants," Moses said from the front seat. He was more amused than angry, remembering when he was once young and overly horny.

"They'll be first rank novitiates at the ritual place whom you can use and abuse."

They continued the rest of the trip in silence. When the Odyssey made the turn toward Assateague Island, Fel wondered just how many people she might have to kill.

The van stopped next to two other cars. Fel and the rest got out and followed a trail to a clearing where portable lights had been set up and a make-shift altar prepared.

Deeply buried memories came back, ones that belonged to the first Felicia Baker. She remembered the first time she/they were here, how she stripped down and climbed willingly on to the altar, waiting for her/their daughter to plunge the knife into her and open the way for a creature from the deepest part of the Pit.

Instead they got me, although they still don't know that.

There was one who did, a survivor of the last time. Fel still remembered the feel of his beating heart in her hands.

"Felicia, it's time," Moses said, coming up behind her. "Prepare yourself and get on the altar. We will have one final communing then send you to glory. Then we will await our master's coming and do his bidding."

He means to strip naked and let them take me, each in his or her own way. Then they'll stab me to death and send me to Hell.

That was not going to happen. Fel decided it was time to end this farce.

She walked up the altar, looked into the expectant faces of the thirteen men and women who now gathered around her. She did not strip. She did not mount the altar.

They want a demon. It's time to give them one.

"Blood was spilled here the last time," she told them. "The blood of your companions. The blood of your Mistress. And most importantly, the blood of Felicia Baker. But it was not by the hand of her daughter that she died. No, a bullet from the gun of an outsider ended her life and opened the way."

Calling on the power within her, Fel let her eyes blaze and her body luminesce. "I came through the open passage, claiming the body of Felicia Baker before any other of my kind could. I am Fel, guardian demon from the Pit, and now servant and companion to the one who brought me forth."

"She speaks the truth," Elva announced. "I feel it. She is from Below." She dropped to her knees before Fel. The others followed. "What is your bidding, Mistress Fel?"

Inwardly Fel smiled and wondered what Simon would make of this? What he would do in this case. But he was not there, she was. And she would follow her nature.

"You want to know the power and glory of Hell. You want to know what awaits you when your time on this mortal plane is over. Very well. Here is the reward which you have earned."

She entered their minds and showed them the true nature of the Pit – the pain, the despair, the endless suffering, and mostly, the utter contempt of its masters for those foolish enough to want to join them in eternal torment. Only once before had she shown others the true nature of Hell, and then only for a second.

That second went by, then another, and then another. Some would have rushed her, others would have run away, still others would have killed themselves and hastened their damnation. Fel did not permit this. They wanted Hell, and she had given it to them. But she was not yet done.

She sought another memory. Not from her current life, and not from the life of Felicia Baker. No, this memory was formed before the worlds began, before the Word had spoken. It was of the Paradise she had betrayed and lost. She let Hell fade from their minds and let Heaven enter.

"This is what I lost. This is what you have given up."

She released them then and as one, they collapsed to the ground. Some were weeping. Some had not survived and had gone on to their fate. Some would reform and some would convince themselves that this had been a trick of some kind and that they had not wasted their lives on a lie.

Fel didn't care. She had done what she had to do. *No,* she corrected herself, *I did what I* chose *to do. What Simon would have done.* Another thought of Paradise flashed through her mind. This time unbidden. It left her with a feeling of peace. A gift perhaps. Maybe when she found Simon or he found her he could explain it.

Coin of the Betrayer

He was known to those who sought him as "Copyright," but that name was seldom uttered. Most of the time he as simply called "the unsub" (by the FBI) or "the killer" (by everyone else). The public at large, including the media, didn't call him anything. They didn't know about him. By consensus, the investigators hunting him kept a lid tighter than Tupperware on his crimes and activities.

Copyright was the most brutal and vicious serial murderer police along the East Coast had ever encountered. It was not just that he had murdered a large number of people. It was how he killed them, and what he did to their bodies before and after death. Once the killer had exhausted the list of known perversions he had gone on to create new ones. When found, what remained of his victims more than sickened experienced police officers and crime scene investigators who had thought they had seen the worse one human being could do to another. Some walked away from their jobs and others were forever after plagued by nightmares. Most of the rest developed a cold spot in their souls and looked forward to the day he was captured.

Other than by their savagery, Charles Odom's crimes were linked by two things. The first was that he always left his victim's head and hands intact. They may not have still been attached to the body, but they were left so that identification could be made. The other was his trademark brand, or rather, his copyright, a "C" contained in a circle.

In private, a task force was formed. It had no name, but it was staffed by the best detectives and forensic investigators from the Federal Government and the jurisdictions most affected by the killer's crimes.

Seven months of hard work followed. There were long nights and lost weekends. There were four divorces and two weddings.

There were dead ends and false trails. In the end, the task force was no closer than when it started. It had the evidence to convict the killer once found. But neither his prints nor his DNA were on file. And if there was a pattern to his crimes the experts could not detect it.

At that point, Special Agent Roy Draper decided to call in an expert. He had worked with the man during the Husk Plague in Baltimore some years back. The man who called himself Sebastian Church had frightened him then and frightened him still but by that time Draper would have dealt with the Devil himself to stop the monster he hunted.

Two weeks passed. Another victim, a young man no older than eighteen, was found off Route 39 in Pennsylvania. After the locals were chased away, Church alone approached the body and knelt by it, his attitude like that a man in prayer. When he stood he consulted a map. He then gave Draper an address, adding, "You should have called me sooner."

There was a smile on Odom's face as the men and women of the task force dragged him out of his hotel room and escorted him to a waiting van. It was likely that he was anticipating the court appearances facing him and the resultant notoriety. His crimes would be revealed and compared to those of the Ripper, Zodiac, and Cleveland's Butcher. Only unlike them, his name would be known and his deeds studied. He would be interviewed by the experts who studied people like him and authors who hoped to profit from his crimes. He would become famous and his name known by all.

He was to be disappointed.

"Are you fully prepared for what you are about to do?" the man known then as Sebastian Church asked the men and women of the task force.

"Like you wouldn't?" asked the detective from Atlantic County, New Jersey.

Church turned to her. "If it were up to me his soul would be suffering in the deepest trench of the Pit right now. But then again, I haven't taken an oath to uphold the laws of my city, state, and country. The breaking of sworn oaths is a serious matter, one that leaves a dark stain on one's soul, no matter how righteous the reason.

So again, are you fully prepared for what you are about to do?"

Having asked the Question and heard the Choice, Sebastian Church walked away, leaving all those remaining to their Fate.

Copyright was killed by a single gunshot at a distance consistent with "shot while trying to escape." Any identification he had was discarded. He was buried as "John Doe" and after his fingerprints and DNA confirmed his crimes, his body was cremated and his ashes scattered.

"Sebastian Church" ceased to exist soon after. The man behind the name went on.

Simon Tombs sat on the balcony of Apartment 1201 of *Le Chateau d'Or* and stared out into the night sky above the Atlantic Ocean. As he wondered what might lay beyond the starry blackness his mostly-reformed demon companion joined him.

Sitting in the recliner next to him Fel asked, "So is this the end of The Followers of the Greater Key?"

"This chapter at least," he replied. "There are others. The Greater Key is worldwide, although the papers left by Magister Reynolds will go a long way toward reducing their number. When we get back home I'll send them where they'll do the most good – Harry in Chicago, Sister Anna in New Orleans, the Holy Office, Jillian at Templar-Mason. They'll know what to do with them."

"Were there any documents in Reynolds's safe that would let us keep this?" Fel waved her arms to indicate the quarters she and Simon were currently "borrowing."

"An outrageously expensive condominium with a 360 view of Ocean City would be nice," Simon admitted. "However, this one has a history of death, mayhem, and being owned by an evil cult."

"So we should let some unsuspecting people buy it?"

"Fel, you're right. Let's see if we can find the ownership papers."

On the way back to Baltimore Simon's phone rang. Since the car he was driving wasn't his – it belonged to the woman who had lured him to Ocean City and who would no longer need it or any other car – Simon had Fel answer for him.

"Hello, Simon Tombs's phone ... Simon, it's someone named Stuart Newman ... No, he can't talk right now. He's driving back to Baltimore in a somewhat stolen car ... Okay, I'll tell him."

"Thank god that wasn't Sergeant Hood. What did Stuart want, Fel?"

"He asked that you call him when you get home, and to remind you that when driving a somewhat stolen car one should obey all traffic laws."

As the latter was good advice, Simon slowed somewhat as he wondered what the curator of the Madison Museum of Antiquities would want with him.

Back in his Baltimore apartment, Simon checked his wards and shields before calling Newman back.

"Stuart, my ... assistant told me you called. Business or pleasure?"

"While it's always a pleasure to see you, Simon, this is more in the way of business. Your kind of business. The kind of business like in that New York museum."

Simon remembered that business well. There had been deaths, deaths that the NYPD attributed to Stuart Newman as he was the only other human in the museum at the time. Simon was in the city at the time, or rather, Sebastian Church was. On hearing of Newman's plight, he investigated on his own and, after one or two run-ins with a certain Detective Christopher Johns, determined that some of the exhibits were not as dead as formerly believed. After some persuasion, and an attack on Detective Johns by a Peruvian mummy, Newman was released. Shortly after that, he took up his current position at the Madison.

"Your collection hasn't started running wild again, has it, Stuart?"

"Nothing that bad, but just as serious. Can you drop by tonight?"

"How about first thing tomorrow morning. My companion and I just got back from some very tiring days in Ocean City. We need to rest, recuperate, and make sure that Kitty has fully digested her latest meal."

"Ocean City? You wouldn't have anything to do with those bodies found on Assateague Island would you?"

"Stuart, I swear to you I was nowhere near that place." Which was the truth. The bodies were Fel's responsibility, even though she had not laid a hand on any of them.

"Tomorrow morning then. Say around nine?"

"A little early for me, but we'll try to make it. What's this all about anyway?"

"Let's just say some coins fell into my possession, coins similar to the one you have."

"Would these be Tyrian shekels and Ptolemaic tetradrachms?"

"Yes, and I need you to authenticate them."

"We'll be there."

"This man knows you. Is he a friend?" Fel asked after Simon had given her some background on Newman.

"He knows me from, well ... before. One of the few who does. And I would say he's more of a colleague than a friend. Despite us both living in Baltimore we haven't kept in touch."

So why does he call me now? Simon thought, even knowing the reason. *I'm one of the few he could call, and the only one he knows.* There was only one other that Simon knew personally, the man who had gifted him his coin. But that man was a wanderer who never stayed in one place very long. Simon decided to call him, even knowing that whatever it was would probably be over before the man got the message.

Going to his study, Simon took a warded box from his bottom desk drawer. Sparks of magic, fatal to anyone but him flew as he opened it. Inside was a similar, smaller box. Again sparks flew as the mage revealed the coin inside.

This is not going to end well, Simon thought. He had the feeling that he was about to step into the wrong story, one that had started over two millennia ago and would not be finished in anyone's lifetime.

Fel was not allowed in the office. It was not that he did not trust her – well, he mostly trusted her – but there were items in there that should not be handled by the untrained, even if she was both

Divine and Demonic.

He took the coin out to her.

Fel was watching one of the streaming channels to which Simon subscribed. This one was premiering a new series adapted from the *Divine Comedy*. In this version celebrities and politicians, living and otherwise, had been substituted for those from Dante's time. This inclusion had, of course, created great controversy and even greater publicity, the most aggrieved being the ones who had been excluded from fictional damnation.

Fel was now on Episode Four, the Third Circle. She had not stopped laughing since the Second Circle. It was, after all, a comedy, to her at least. She was having such a good time that Simon hated to disturb her.

"Fel, would you please turn that off. I have something to show you." She shut off the TV, turning to her master who sat across from her. "What can you tell me about this?" He put the coin on the table.

Fel gasped. Simon could tell by the look on her face and the trembling of her body that she wanted to flee the room.

"I know of these," she said once she had recovered from the shock. "They were talked about deep in the Pit. It is one of the coins of the Betrayer. There is only the one?"

Simon nodded. "Here, at least. The man who called may have more. How many I don't know. Can you tell me anything about them?"

Her face pale, Fel nodded. "They are part of the price of a slave, part of the price of …" She struggled to get the words out. "… The Christ. They must never be gathered together."

"And what would happen if they were?" Simon asked, thinking, *Nothing good I'm sure. That's the way stories like this go.*

"It is said that if all thirty coins were brought together, they could be used to buy a soul out of Hell."

"And why would the unholy ones want to let even one soul go. They get so upset when I do it."

"I … do not know. But I know it is so."

Simon picked up his coin. Taking it back to his study, he replaced it for the night in its box and that in the larger box. Returning to Fel, he said, "I'd like you to come with me tomorrow. No telling what may happen when things with this much potential for mischief are involved."

The next morning, about nine, with no one else there to bother them, Newman let Simon and Fel into the Madison through a side entrance and led them to his office. He gestured them to seats in front of his desk.

"Forgive me, Miss. We have not been introduced."

"I'm Fel," she said, "we spoke on the phone."

"Ah yes, and how are you related to Simon? By blood, I hope."

Fel gave Newman a smile and brought up a little fire to her eyes. "I'm his personal demon."

"Ah yes," Newman said, not sure whether to believe her or not. To Simon he said, "You always did meet the most interesting people. But to business. Miss Fel, would you please excuse us. Feel free to look around. There's nothing here that's all that breakable, just stuff that we can't or shouldn't display. Simon, I'll get the coins."

Newman disappeared into an alcove, returned with a battered tin dispatch box with the name "Watson" painted on its lid.

"You should let me ward that," Simon offered.

"This is a museum, Simon. All the good stuff is out there." Newman looked up to see Fel holding a piece of pottery.

"Be careful of that, my dear. It's ancient Egyptian, very ancient. Possible the oldest thing in the building."

"I doubt that," Simon said, knowing that Fel was much, much older than Egypt.

Newman opened the tin box. "And now, Simon, what you came to see." Newman took out a chamois bag.

"I got the last of these from that shop in Istanbul," he said. "You remember that one, the blackbird and the granddaughter of the fat man."

Simon shook his head. "They keep looking but they'll never find it."

The two men exchanged a glance. They alone knew where that dream was hidden and had vowed never to mention its location, not even to each other.

From the bag, Newman spilled out silver coins, each one at least two millennia old. Simon did a quick count as he felt his own coin begin to warm in the watch pocket of his pants.

Simon picked each one up, looked at it, and put it back on the table, counting as he did.

"Twenty-six, twenty-seven, twenty-eight, twenty-nine. Fel, could you step over here a minute."

Fel approached the table and gasped. If she had been still been holding the Egyptian jug she would have dropped it and destroyed a piece of history.

"Well?" Simon asked. "Are these are the genuine coins?"

She nodded, her face pale, the demon part of her wanting to gather up the coins from the table and flee but knowing it could not. The guardian part of her wanted to do something deadly but refrained, knowing she could always act later.

"How does she know?"

"Trust me, Stuart, of all people Fel would know. Fel, might we have trouble from … Below?"

"There is no doubt great excitement in the Pit right now. Powers are forming, armies of the Fallen might be gathering. Master, this is not good."

Simon agreed. A naturally suspicious soul, he began to suspect that his old friend wanted something more than authentication.

With a smile he really wasn't feeling, Simon picked up the coins and dropped them in the chamois bag, counting as he did so. "Twenty-seven, twenty-eight, and twenty-nine. Relax, Fel. As you can see, Stuart is one short."

"But not for long, Simon," Newman said. "When you give me yours I will have all thirty pieces of silver."

"And what makes you think I brought it with me?"

"Because I know you, Simon Tombs. I knew you when you were Sebastian Church. You never could resist the grand gesture, a piece of showmanship, the daring of Fate with a smile and a nod and a wink. You have it. You couldn't not bring it, and if I had one less coin yours would be on my desk right now."

He's right, Simon admitted to himself. *I should have left it home. But too late now.* Still, he wasn't worried. He had a plan. He just hoped it would work.

"Why?" Several questions with that one word. Why do you want my coin? What do you plan to do with it? How do you plan to get it from me? Who do you want to ransom from Perdition?

Simon felt a disturbance in the supernatural plane. Fel was right, forces were gathering. Demons were not known for their patience and he worried about his companion. He could sense Fel's agitation and hoped she would not do anything … permanent. He did not want to explain a dead museum curator to Caitlin Hood. Then again, having the twenty-nine coins seized by the police and locked up as evidence would be a good way to take them out of circulation.

If only I had established an alibi, he thought as Newman began to explain.

"My father left home when I just a boy. My mother and I would hear from him, but only occasionally. He always had his own business to attend to, or so he told us. After a while … nothing. We stopped hearing from him. My mother divorced him, remarried, and I took my new father's name.

"Much later I was arrested for those New York deaths. Yes, you cleared me, but not before they fingerprinted me and took a DNA sample. About a month later I received a call from now Sergeant Christopher Johns. My DNA was a filial match to DNA in the national database. DNA that matched that of a serial killer who was killed while trying to escape arrest and was never identified. Johns told me what he could. The Freedom of Information Act told me the rest. I believe you were there for my father's execution."

"Charles Odom," Simon said. "Copyright. A monster who belongs in Hell."

"He was my father. Not much of one but I loved him. He deserved justice. He deserved a chance at redemption.

"I heard about the legend of the coins, what together they might do. Finding the first was the hardest. After that, well, I find these sort of things for a living. And now, I'm ready to give my father his chance to repent, or failing that, his chance at revenge."

"And how are you going to do that? I have the last coin."

"You're going to give it to me."

"Or else," Simon said. "You're supposed to end that sentence with 'or else.' It's in the bad guys' rule book. And then I ask, 'Or else what?' and then you threaten death, destruction, or the cancellation of my museum membership. Now let's try that again."

"Damn you, Simon."

"It's been tried. It didn't take. And now if you'll excuse me, Fel and I are leaving."

Simon stood. Fel made a point of getting between him and Newman.

"You know, Simon, I did learn something from that New York mess. I learned just how dangerous items from the past can be. There are some in this museum. My 'or else' – the coin or I turn them loose on the city. You and the Blonde from Hell might be able to stop them, but not before they cause more deaths than my father ever did, or will."

Fel took a step toward Newman. "No, Fel, he's right. We've been outplayed. Stuart here will get my coin. He's won this battle. We'll win the next one, even if I have to beg favors from people I really don't want to owe. Stuart, do I have your word that if I give you my coin you'll disable whatever nasty surprises this museum holds?"

Newman paused, seemed to stare into space for a moment then said, "Done. As soon as your coin is in this bag, they'll be no danger."

Reaching into his watch pocket, Simon took out his coin. "Open the bag, Stuart," he said, ready to drop it in.

"Not so fast, Simon. Open your hand."

Simon did, revealing the coin and the silver dollar he had planned to drop into the bag in its place.

"Really, Simon?"

"You would have been disappointed if I hadn't tried."

"True. Now drop the real one in."

Simon deliberately placed the silver dollar on the desk. Then, holding the Betrayer's coin between thumb and forefinger, he held it over the chamois bag.

He asked the Question. "Are you sure you want to do this, Stuart?"

"Yes."

The Choice made, Simon dropped the coin.

"Thank you, Simon. You should go now. What I have to do next is best done in private. And from what I've heard, the ones that would claim the coins may not come if you are present."

Simon and Fel left the way they entered. "But, Simon ..."

"Fel, be quiet and keep walking. And for the rest of the day, it's best we stay out in public and walk by as many surveillance cameras as we can, maybe even have lunch with the mayor and dinner with the archbishop. I think you and he would have lots to talk about."

Shortly after Simon and Fel left the museum, Stuart Newman prepared his office. The furniture was moved, the carpet rolled up, the proper symbols drawn on the hardwood floor. He burned the incense, said the words, then cursed the names of the Three. Despite the afternoon sun coming through his window, the room grew dark. Shadows appeared where there should be none. The shades had no form, not in this world, but they did have mouths which showed sharp teeth when they smiled. And smile they did for they had long awaited this.

"What would have of us?" asked several tongues at once.

"The return of the one known as Charles Odom."

Multiple voices replied. "He is deep below, a great sinner. What price will you pay?"

"The price of the ... a slave. The price of your Enemy." Newman threw the chamois bag toward the nearest shadow.

The mayor was unavailable and the archbishop was in Rome. Simon settled for heading north with no destination in mind but intending to drive through as many toll booths as possible, even if that meant getting on and off the New Jersey Turnpike several times.

It was a quiet trip, with Fel alternately seething and pouting.

Simon had forbidden her to mention the coin and she wanted to speak of nothing else. He finally decided that it was safe to turn south and they stopped at Mamie's Café in Aberdeen for dinner. They took a table in the back and spoke in low voices.

Midway through a plate-sized cheeseburger Fel could not take it any longer.

"How could you, Simon? We would have stopped that man's monsters eventually. Many would have died horribly but their deaths would be nothing compared to what those below might do now that they have His price. How could you give up your coin like that?"

Simon looked at his now less than demonic companion and smiled. It was a smile that Fel had seen before, one that told her that he had done something clever and just had to tell someone.

Holding up a seemingly empty hand he asked, "You mean this?" An ancient silver coin hit the table.

As soon as it left Simon's possession Fel knew it for one of the Thirty. "But how?" she asked. "I saw you drop it in the bag."

"Yes, I know," he answered smugly. "And drop it in I did. That was the deal I agreed to. And Stuart knew me too well not to suspect that I would try to trick him. I brought more than one silver dollar with me, just in case he had the remaining twenty-nine coins. When I put *his* coins back in the bag I switched one out and dropped in one of the dollars instead. The cheat was done before the deal was made."

"So when he tries to buy his father's release ..."

"He will not have the purchase price. Do you see now why I wanted to be over the hills and very far away? Now finished your burger, there's rice pudding for dessert."

A smoky tentacle claimed the chamois bag, drew it into itself. There followed a combined shriek that shattered every window of the office and every piece of glass therein.

"You would try to cheat us?" the voices howled. The smiles faded but the teeth remained and moved forward.

As he was enveloped in darkness, as his flesh was slowly ripped from his body and devoured, Stuart Newman's last words on this plane and the words he was destined to repeat for the long and painful descent to that level of the Pit reserved for betrayers were "Damn you, Simon."

A few days later, with Fel at the bar drinking yet another of Murphy's alcoholic concoctions, Simon caught up with an old friend.

"Sorry we were late. Fel and I are still trying to convince a certain police sergeant that we had nothing to do with the death of a museum curator."

"I was later," his friend said. "Had I received your message earlier …"

Simon shook his head. "Nothing would have changed." He studied the man across from him. His friend had the darkened skin of someone who had spent much of his long life, a life much longer than Simon's, in the Middle East. And his voice still had traces of the small Judean town where he was born. There was a rope scar around his neck that he did not try to hide.

The man looked over at Fel. Over his many years he had known many women and seen many more. This did not lessen his appetite for them.

"She's going to betray you, you know that."

Simon nodded. "It's a possibility."

"More than that. Take it from someone who knows betrayal."

"And forgiveness," Simon reminded him.

The man rubbed his neck, as if feeling the bite of the noose cutting into him once again. "That last minute as I hung there, when I finally realized what I had done and regretted it, the branch broke and I knew. It wasn't a bright light on the Damascus Road but it was enough."

"So why don't you move on?"

"He may have forgiven me, but I haven't forgiven myself. One day, maybe."

"The wandering Jew."

"You're only off by one syllable."

It was an old joke between the two. There was a pause then,

"So they're gone?" the man asked.

"Most of them, down to the Pit, where they will be a constant source of war, dissension, and betrayal."

"Almost as if you had planned it."

Simon smiled. "I wish. That reminds me." Simon reached into his pocket. "This once belonged to you." A silver coin only slightly older than the man hit the table. The man hesitated before picking it up.

"They were only mine for a short time. I still remember throwing them at the feet of the priests." He returned the coin to the table. "Keep it. It will be safer with you."

"Don't worry about that. I have another." Simon pulled another coin from his pocket, the twin of the first. "I had several silver dollars with me. When I saw that Stuart wasn't paying close attention as I was dropping his coins in the bag I went for two."

Signs of Death

Ginny London had had many lovers, but only one true love. She met him in England, back in the 70's. Like many in these stories, she had a different name back then. She was only eighteen and had just discovered the mysteries of the occult and the pleasures of the flesh. Shortly after these discoveries, she met Thomas Defreyne, who was adept at both and was willing to instruct a willing student. Ginny was very willing and for the next five years they lived and loved while fighting this monster and that beast and the occasional mad wizard out to destroy the world or open a portal to release some thing that would.

All of the threats they faced failed. There were some near things and some close calls, but Thomas always seemed to have a trick or two up his sleeve, along with a very sharp knife. Each time they came out of it whole, with only minor or repairable injuries.

Each time but the last.

In quiet times, Ginny often thought back to when she was someone else, when she was young and in love and living in the city whose name she had adopted as her own. Inevitably, she'd think about that last time.

There was a baby in a cage, one with dark, shining, red eyes and very sharp teeth. It was, Thomas told her, a manifestation of something far worse. One that, unless dealt with, would leave England with a new coastline and a need for a new capital.

"So when do we go after it?" she had asked him.

"We don't. I do. Your job will be to get the Royals to safety. If all goes wrong they'll provide a sense of stability."

"All of them?"

Thomas smiled then, the last one he ever gave her. "The Queen, the heir, and a spare, at least." He paused a moment, then said, "This time, darling, well, there may be no coming back."

He then gave her a kiss, one that had goodbye in it, and was gone.

Thomas saved the day, but she never saw him again.

She tried to carry on but soon found that she could no longer stay in the country that had cost her the only man she loved. She moved to the States, changed her name, and opened a bookstore in Baltimore, Maryland; a city Thomas had often mentioned, describing it as a pleasant place to live, however dangerous it might be.

The first body was discovered in Southeast Baltimore, by the Pagoda in Patterson Park. The victim was a white female who had suffered several stab wounds of the torso, one of which ripped open her abdomen. Her throat had also been cut, two deep knife wounds almost severing her neck.

Other than her killer, there were no witnesses to Carmella Skinner's death. There were no fingerprints or DNA on her body, and nothing was found that would place anyone but her on the scene.

Everyone who saw the body – patrol officers, detectives, crime scene technicians, Medical Examiners – all had the same thought. None spoke this thought aloud for fear of summoning the devil that might be in their midst. After reading the case folder and viewing the crime scene photos, Detective Sergeant Caitlin Hood felt a shiver run down her spine and hoped that there would be no need to rebuild a bridge she had not too recently burned.

When the bells of her front door rang Ginny looked up to see Simon Tombs walk into her shop. Not for the first time did she notice the resemblance between him and her one true love. This resemblance often led to her wonder about magic and its possibilities, but she knew in her heart that Thomas, wherever and whoever he might be now, was lost to her. Simon, she had decided long ago, was himself and no other. But each time he came into London's Books she sighed and wished that she and Thomas had left England, London, and the Royals to their fate.

"Ginny," he said with his ever-present smile, "how's my favorite bookseller? Please tell me you called because some of the books I ordered came in."

Ginny shook her head. "Nothing yet."

"Not even the new *From the Shadows* magazine?"

"I don't know how you read that thing. It gives me nightmares."

Another smile. "I think that's the idea. So how can I help?"

"First of all, Tir na Con is coming up. Can you man the table again this year?"

"Delighted. But are sure you can't make it. The Gentry will be disappointed."

"I'm getting too old for a three-day convention, not to mention the drive. Why they had to move to the Bay I'll never know."

"For the convenience of our, shall we say, out of town visitors. But don't worry, I'll be glad to fill in. I'll take Fel. She can help. With her looks and in the right costume, we'll double last year's sales."

Ginny got a worried look on her face. "Are you sure you want *her* and *them* to meet. You know what might happen."

"Yes, I do. Might be fun. But I promise that she'll be on her best behavior. Now then, what else do you need?"

Ginny reached under the counter, brought up a book with a faux-leather binding, and handed it to Simon. Taking it from her hand, he examined it.

"Chandler's *The Smell of Fear*, Heron Books 1981 edition. I have the whole set at home."

"Look at the Chandler illustration in front."

Simon opened the book. Opposite the title page was a pencil drawing of the author. Below this was the signature "Raymond Chandler."

"If Chandler had not died in 1959 I'd swear this was genuine."

"There are some who would still swear it. Simon, have you ever heard of Josephine Brooks?"

"Didn't Eve Arden play her on television?"

Ginny's first answer was a sigh. Her second was "That was *Our Miss Brooks*, whose first name was Constance. No, Simon, Josephine Brooks claims to be a physic who can channel dead authors. She holds signings and charges five dollars a signature."

"Not a bad price. There are those who would charge more, and those who would pay more, much more. Why the interest?'

Ginny looked toward the signing area in the back. "She did a signing in Philadelphia that was a big success. I'm hosting one this Saturday. I'm hoping you can be there."

"So I can tell you whether this Miss Brooks is the real thing or just a highly skilled forger with a very good memory?" Ginny nodded. "And which are you hoping for, my dear?"

"A large turnout where I sell lots of books written by dead people." Then she added, "And if she can really summon the dead, well, there are some questions I'd like answered."

"The past is passed, Ginny," Simon said quietly. "And it is not wise to drag it into the present where so many things have changed."

"Maybe you're right … Simon." She had almost called him "Thomas", and wondered what he would have done or said if she had. "Well, I've got plans to make and you've got books to buy. There's a new Camelot anthology I think you'll like. And Saturday, when you come, plan on using the back door. I'm hoping there'll be a line out the front. And leave *her* at home. You might trust *her*, but I don't."

Like Carmella Skinner, Mara Chang was a prostitute. Her body was found when the lift truck hoisted the dumpster behind the Travel Plaza hotel. Mara's body had been under it.

Mara appeared to have suffered the same kinds of wound as had Carmella– deep cuts to the throat, her abdomen ripped open. As the officers, crime scene people, and homicide detectives viewed her body in the cold light of day, they all knew that the monster they had feared was among them. Still, no one dared utter the defining words they were all thinking. Instead, most of them said a silent, selfish prayer that leaving Mara's body behind the Travel Plaza meant that her killer was on his way out of town and soon to be someone else's problem.

It was not until the autopsy that the Medical Examiner discovered that her uterus was missing.

As she read the case folder, as she looked at the crime scene photos and compared them to the ones from the first murder, Caitlin

Hood's hand almost reached out to the smartphone on her desk. On that phone was a number she should have deleted months ago, one that would connect to an attractive (even to her), self-assured man who was too clever for anyone's good. She thought of this man and of his too-young-looking-for-her age "companion," the blonde who sniffed death and who both haunted and blessed the detective's dreams. She once desired this woman, and might still again, even after witnessing her kill a man while leaving no mark the medical examiner could find.

Caitlin picked up the phone, found the number, almost pressed "Call." Then she put it back down on the desk. *We don't need him,* she told herself. *This isn't Gotham, and he's no dark knight. We solve our own murders.*

Ginny had been right about the line. To her delight, it stretched out the door and down the block. The other merchants didn't seem to mind. On the theory that a rising tide lifts all boats, they got busy trying to entice the waiting book lovers into their own shops, the more enterprising among them walking the line and hawking their wares.

To Simon's disappointment, Miss Brooks (as Simon could not help but think of her) looked nothing like Eve Arden did when the show was on. She was instead a large woman of sixty-something, who was winning her struggle against the inevitable with a sensible diet, regular exercise, and a very professional and expensive dye job. Simon hoped that he would look as good as she if he ever decided to let himself age.

As Miss Brooks prepared herself for the onslaught, Ginny posted "The Rules" where all might see them.

Deceased authors only.

For every book of yours you wish signed you must buy one from the shop.

All books must have been published at least two years after the author's death.

Maximum of eight books signed.

Miss Brooks nodded that she was ready, and the more or

less orderly line moved forward. As books got signed and Ginny accepted payment for the books she sold, Simon watched the lady who wielded the pen.

Each time it was the same. Someone would approach Miss Brooks, their book opened to the title page. Miss Brooks's eyes would close but a moment and when they opened it was as if she were someone else for just the brief time it took to put a name to the paper.

Sometimes this "someone" seemed in pain, as if they had just suffered a great loss. At others, they seemed relieved, as if a horrible burden had been lifted from them. And each time either happened, Simon, his senses opened, felt a surge of power.

It took him six or seven customers before he figured out what was happening. Still, he needed to test his theory. He waited for a break in the line.

Five more people got their books signed before it came. A delay at Ginny's register for a charge to go through caused a gap into which he stepped. He had but one book, one he had brought from home. It was a new retelling of the Beanstalk story, this time with a female "Jac." The author who had long ago written the story for his daughter had passed on before the book was published. Simon decided to get his copy signed.

He presented the book. Miss Brooks closed her eyes. When she opened them there was a look of confusion, then he heard,

"Welcome … to the … big fat, wonderful world of … wherever this is." The author, for Simon had no doubt it was he, then said, "I'm in a bookstore so this still must be heaven. Oh, it's you. What have you … so it did come out. Nice job." He put pen to paper, made his usual scrawl, and was gone.

With a whispered "Goodbye, CJ," Simon stepped out of line, all doubts about Miss Brooks now gone.

About1 a.m. on the morning of the signing, an officer on patrol in the Central District looked down Lovegrove Street and saw one person standing and another on the ground. Calling for back-up, Officer Denice Winter hit her lights and siren and turned her cruiser into the alley-wide street. One of the people ran. Officer Winter would have given chase but for the other person, who was on the ground not moving. She called for the medics, got out of her car, and rushed to the victim.

Joyce Reid was beyond help. A single knife slash had opened her carotid artery and she had bled out even before Officer Winter got to her. Realizing that this was one person she could not save, she looked in the direction the killer had fled and wished, not for the first time, that officers in the BPD rode with partners.

Slashing attacks on prostitutes had become the highest priority. Within minutes of her calling it in, the scene was soon filled with sergeants, lieutenants, and members of the command staff. Fortunately, Caitlin Hood beat most of them there.

"Quickly now," she said to the shaken officer, "before the brass monkeys arrive. What happened?"

Upset at witnessing a murder, upset that the killer had gotten away, Denice Winter was still all cop. She gave Caitlin a clear, concise statement after which the homicide sergeant packed her into a patrol car. "Take her to HQ. Get her showered and in fresh clothes. Bag the ones she has on, some of the victim's blood is on them. Then lock her in an interview room and don't let anyone, I mean anyone, in to see her unless it's me or Payne."

To Winter she said, "Denice, you did good. This might be our first break. Now until Detective Payne or I come to talk to you, all I need you to do is remember all that you saw tonight."

With Winter gone and safe from those who would do nothing but tell her what she should have done, Caitlin was able to concentrate on the crime scene.

"Just a single slash this time, Sergeant," said the Crime Lab Tech who had bent down to take a close-up photo of the wound. "Looks like Winter interrupted him this time."

Something about the killer being interrupted sounded familiar. Then it clicked for Sergeant Hood and she suddenly thought of a deep path through a dark forest. She knew what, or who, or maybe both, they were dealing with.

He's still out there and he's not finished.

"10-13" she all but shouted into her radio. "I need Foxtrot in the air over the Central, centering on the scene location. Get me all available units to search the alleys, streets, and anywhere else they can think of. And see if the Crime Scene Unit has that new drone of theirs up and flying. The Killer's going for two."

She then stripped the scene, leaving only officers at either end of the street and one standing guard over the crime scene tech.

"He's on foot. He can't be far." This was a much a wish and prayer than anything else. "Double up. Find him. Stop him. Remember, he's a got a knife and knows how to use it." Then she joined the search herself, wishing she had an attractive, self-assured man and a sexy, killer blonde at her side.

They did not find the killer. But they did find his work some blocks away at Morton and Oliver, on the first level of a parking garage that had closed for renovations. Like Carmella Skinner and Mara Chang before her, Reba Armstrong's throat was severed and abdomen ripped open. It was clear that organs were missing, which ones only an autopsy could determine.

A dual investigation, the questioning and protecting of Officer Winter, dealing with the "what-ifs" and the "why nots" and the "why didn't yous", there would be no sleep for her that night and probably not the next one either. Standing over the second victim's body, Caitlin Hood finally gave a name to the killer. The only name she could.

"Jack" she whispered, then she slowly walked away.

"She seems to me to be some kind of necromancer," Simon said to Ginny after the event was over. Miss Brooks had stayed past the stated time to make sure everyone had their "autographs." Surprisingly, given the crowd, there had been very little trouble. Simon had had to intervene only twice. Once when a woman wanted a Stephen King book signed, insisting that the author had died in 1999 when he was hit by a minivan and that all books published under his name after that were written by ghostwriters. However appropriate this would have been for a horror writer, Simon convinced the woman that King was alive then Ginny managed to sell her a Jack Ketchum book.

The other incident was the same in reverse. Miss Brooks brought forth Elvis Presley to sign a biography written about him, which caused a man waiting in line to proclaim her a fraud as the King was still alive and running a Cracker Barrel in Alabama. Simon had to escort him out before he could get his copy of *The Spirit: Femmes Fatales* "signed" by Will Eisner.

"You think so?" asked Ginny, who was happily counting her day's take while Simon cleaned up.

Simon nodded. "She's calling them down from Heaven and up from Hell for purposes of her own," he said. "In the process, she's causing the former the pain of sudden separation from the Divine and giving the latter relief from their punishment. That's sound like necromancy to me."

"So what are you going to do about it?" Ginny left off counting her money to arrange a special display of stock books Miss Brooks has signed as a "thank you" for Ginny hosting her signing.

"Not a thing." At Ginny's look of surprise, Simon said. "She's not out to rule the world or punish her enemies or anything even remotely nefarious. She's just trying to make a little, or rather, judging from how many books she signed at five dollars a throw, a lot of money. And I'm sure that the Powers That Be both Above and Below are aware of what she's doing. If it bothers them, let them stop her."

Clean up was done. Ginny closed the shop, and she and Simon had a late tea. Before he left, she gifted him with a signed copy of *Meet the Tiger*. "This one's genuine," she assured him.

Simon kissed her on each cheek, once as a thank you and once in farewell. He then left the shop.

Looking right from London's Books, he saw a familiar being waiting a half block away. It was a plain looking woman, her hair a non-descript brown. Her figure was covered by a bulky sweater, which may have served to conceal a weight problem. Her jeans were faded and somewhat worn at the knee. Her feet were in sandals and did not quite touch the sidewalk.

Simon looked to his left and was not surprised to see a shadow where none should be. It had dark shining red eyes and a smile with very sharp teeth.

Caught between the wicked and the divine, Simon looked right, then left, then right again. Finally, he said firmly, "No. You two work this out." Then he crossed the street, flagged down a taxi, and went home more than half convinced that they'd be waiting for him when he got there.

Someone was waiting, but it wasn't an envoy from either of the Powers That Be.

Simon was greeted at his door by Fel who immediately said, "Shhh. We have a visitor."

"Just one?" Simon looked around. "Where is she, he, it?"

Fel pointed to her bedroom. "She's in there. It's Sergeant Hood."

Simon smiled a smile as devilish as any his somewhat-demon companion had seen in her millennia Below. "Why, Fel, you little devil, pun intended. Is Caitlin asleep? Is she dressed? And how did all this happen?"

Fel sighed. She knew that the man she sometimes called "master" would react like that. Oddly, he didn't seem jealous. Amused, maybe, but not jealous.

"Yes, she's asleep. And yes, she's dressed. And no, nothing like what you're imaging happened. She arrived about two hours ago, barely on her feet and completely worn out. When I saw her condition I took her into my room. She collapsed on the bed and went right out."

"Did she say anything?"

"Just, 'Jack. Tell Simon.'"

Simon thought a moment, then opened the door to his apartment. He looked up and down the hallway. Seeing nothing there he closed the door again.

"Sorry. I'm expecting company. Possibly an old friend of yours and its opposite number. But that's a different problem, I hope. In stories like these they tend to merge. Now then, if I know Caitlin, she's been working nonstop on a major case, probably that serial killer I've heard rumors about. Jack, you say she said. That might mean … oh, I hope I'm wrong."

Simon went into action. "Get dinner on the table. That paprika chicken we had last night. There's enough for three. And the strongest coffee we've got, the kind Zeke's makes you sign a waiver for before you buy it. Caitlin's going to be a bad mood when she wakes up and it's best I do it gradually."

Caitlin Hood was sleeping the sleep of the exhausted. No dreams, just utter and complete forgetfulness mixed with total relaxation. That is, she was, until from a distance she heard,

"Katie, Katie, rise and shine. It's time to go to class. You wouldn't want to be late for your first day in detective school."

I know that voice, her dream self said. *But no one calls me Katie except …*

Reality hit her harder than she liked. One moment she was blissfully unaware and the next … she was in bed and Simon Tombs was talking to her. *Oh god, make it not so!*

Then she realized that she was still fully dressed and Simon was talking to her from a distance, and not lying next to her.

"Tombs? Where?"

"Relax, Caitlin, you're in Fel's bed. Someplace I've never been by the way. She told me that when you arrived you were about to fall over, and since I've always told her that an unconscious police officer is a bad thing to have on one's living room floor she put you in here. Now, what's this about Jack the Ripper?"

Over dinner and coffee that should be illegal, Caitlin explained about the four murders and how they fit into the Ripper's pattern. "I think he even planned the interruption. The woman was probably already dead and he just waited for someone to spot him."

Simon nodded. "And the fifth is yet to come. It will be the messiest and, being indoors, the hardest to find. You'll need more officers than you have to search all of the city's vacant buildings, assuming he doesn't kill his Mary Jane Kelly in a Route 40 motel where she'll be found in a day or two. Or in her home, to found by neighbors or her family."

"Tombs, I know. Which is why I've come to you. I know I have no right to ask, not after the way I treated you."

"Horribly," Fel said from across the table.

"Now, Fel ..."

"No, she's right. You warned me that I'd be walking a dark path. I didn't listen and blamed you for what I found there. I'm sorry. What can I do to make it up to you?"

Fel uttered something like a low growl. To forgive is to be divine, and she was not quite there yet. Simon, however, merely said,

"You can start by calling me 'Simon' again. Now then, no doubt you've checked to see if this Ripper pattern has played out in other cities?" Caitlin nodded. "How many?"

"Just one, two weeks ago in Philadelphia. We're trading crime scene photos and case folders now."

Philadelphia. Ginny had mentioned that city. Miss Brooks had been there. Miss Brooks the psychic, Miss Brooks the unwitting (maybe) necromancer who could bring the dead back from Hell.

What was I saying about stories merging? Simon thought. To Caitlin he said, "There may have been others. Police don't like to admit to having a serial killer in their midst, much less letting him get away. I'll get you a list tomorrow. You arrange to get me access to one of the scenes, the garage would be best."

Caitlin nodded and got up from the table. "I'll take care of it. And thanks ... Simon." She looked at her phone, checked the time. "I should be going."

"Do you have too?" Simon asked with an impish grin. "My bed's bigger than Fel's. There's room for three, or two and a very interested observer."

Fel looked at Caitlin and cast a mild glamour that slightly tempted her, one the detective shook off with a smile (and a barely concealed sigh).

"I'll call you tomorrow," she said.

As soon as Detective Hood left, Simon called Ginny. "Can you get me a list of signings our Miss Brooks did before coming to Baltimore? And her next few stops just in case?"

"In case of what, Simon? Is there a problem?"

"Isn't there always? Let's just say hang on to those books she signed for you. They might be the last of their kind."

The next day Ginny emailed the list to Simon who in turn forwarded it to Detective Hood. Caitlin called back within two hours.

"The last five before Baltimore were Indianapolis, Cincinnati, Columbus, Pittsburgh, and Philadelphia. It took some poking, prodding, calls from the Chief of Detectives, and finally, the dual threats of a federal investigation and a call to *60 Minutes* before Columbus and Pittsburgh fessed up. We already knew about Philadelphia and the other two swear that nothing like Jack has ever happened."

"Do we believe them?"

"I do."

"Good enough for me, Caitlin. What about access to a crime scene?"

"Set up for eight this evening."

"See you then."

After he hung up, Simon sat at his kitchen table, drinking sweet tea and thinking out loud. "Someone in Columbus presented Miss Brooks a Jack the Ripper book and asked that Jack himself sign it, much the same way that Elvis book was signed. Jack was called back from Hell and somehow managed to stay, tucked away in a part of Miss Brooks's mind. Or it could have happened before Columbus and he wasn't able to take her over until then. Either way, now at every stop she makes Jack comes out to play."

Fel had been listening to Simon's monologue. "So what's the next step? Find her and kill her?"

"Would it were that easy. Miss Brooks may be an innocent in all this, blissfully unaware of what's going on. On the other hand, she may know and not be able to do anything about it except to dispose of the bloody clothing. Or contact with Jack may have turned her into a serial killer. We won't know until we locate her. And if she does wind up dead, will that return Jack to the Pit, or will he just find another host?"

"How are you going to find her? Track her from the last murder scene?"

Simon shook his head. "That might show me where the evil lies but not the woman. I have something else in mind." He looked at his watch. "Some hours yet. I should have time. I'll be in my study."

"Simon," Fel said in a worried voice, "don't use the bridge. They'll be waiting for you."

"I'm sure they will," he answered with a smile. "So let's save that for a real emergency. If you'll excuse me?"

Simon shut himself away, taking with him the book he had signed the day before. "I need your help one last time, old friend," he said and opened the slim volume.

The signature on the title page was that of the author, but it was made by the woman who had called him down from Heaven. Calling up his power, he put his finger on the page.

It was easy, this time. He had met Miss Brooks, had shaken her hand and had asked her to use her powers on his behalf. The universe did not need much coaxing to reveal her to his open senses.

Memories of the modern day bard were the first to flood his mind. Simon filtered them out, leaving just impressions of Josephine Brooks.

Carefully he probed, wanting only the woman, not quite ready to face Jack, if indeed they were two separate entities.

There was not much to Miss Brooks. An ordinary childhood, no great traumas or tragedies, no major triumphs or failures. The discovery of her power in her late twenties, the thing that made her special. Her decision on how to use it. Minor conventions and book fairs, then larger ones. Establishing a following, then a reputation, going on a national tour, finally a success.

With Jack still sleeping, or else awake and hiding and plotting nasty surprises, Simon looked for her presence in Baltimore, finding her in an Airbnb in Canton.

Enough.

Simon broke contact and went out to Fel who was in the living room reading Newton's *Encyclopedia of Serial Killers*.

"Use me," she said, looking up from the Jack the Ripper entry.

"In what way?" he asked, suspecting the answer.

"As bait. Set me up as the Ripper's fifth victim. He will not survive the encounter."

"Miss Brooks definitely would not, and I could find no trace of him in her psyche. His spirit is riding her. But I do have a job for you."

Taking out his phone Simon showed Fel a picture he had taken of Miss Brooks at the signing. Then he gave her the address of the woman's Airbnb.

"If she leaves there, follow her. Take your phone. I'll keep track of you on mine. Get close enough for her to see you if she looks. Take no action unless another's life is at risk. If so, then do what you must. Just make sure …"

"I know, don't get caught."

"That my girl."

After Fel left, Simon almost returned to his study. Instead, he decided the balcony was better suited to what he had to do.

First, as always, he looked over at the Starry Night hotel. Then he looked at the space above it and from there up into the heavens. Then he looked down at the street, imagining that he could see through all the way down to the traditional location of fiery punishment.

"Okay, you two," he said quietly, sure that his intended audience could hear him. "This is what we're going to do."

Eight o'clock. At this time of year, just about the time evening slowly fades into night. Like dawn, sunset was a time of power, neutral territory for Light and Dark. Except that this time of day, the Dark was in the ascendancy. Normally Simon did these things at dawn, but that night darkness suited his purpose.

Reba Armstrong's body had been removed but her blood still stained the cement of the garage's second level. It had been spilled with evil intent, and Simon hoped to trace that evil back to its source.

"Where's the girl?" Sergeant Hood asked. Was that a touch of disappointment in her voice, Simon wondered.

"You mean Fel? Despite her appearance, she's hardly a girl, but

I think you know that. I think you suspect who and what she is. But to answer your question, she may be joining us later, at least, I hope so. If not, it's possible that this problem is solved leaving us with a host of other ones."

Simon sat on the cold garage floor. "What do you need me to do?" Caitlin asked.

"Wait, watch, and guard me against physical threats. Have your officers withdraw and protect the access points. No sense risking everyone. And tell them if they see a large, sixtyish woman who is being closely followed by the female of both our dreams, let them pass."

"Is this woman … Jack?"

"Yes. No. Maybe. It's complicated. And in case you're wondering why I didn't lead you to her, it's important that she come to us – freely, and of her own will. Now if you'll excuse, I have to try to pull a rabbit out of the hat."

In Simon's mind, a squirrel reminded him that that trick never works, but he stopped listening to talking animals since a run-in with a large, white rabbit.

Closing his eyes, Simon opened his senses to everything around him. The garage and all those who used it. Daytime parking for school and work. In the evening for dinner and the nearby dance clubs. At night, for licit and illicit romantic interludes as well as other, less legal activities.

But that was just setting the scene. Slowly he narrowed his attention to the blood in front of him, its appearance, the coppery smell he could almost taste in the air above it, the way dried portions of it had started to flake off.

Blood is life, and blood is death. It is part of the essence of a person, part of the song that is unique to them. And having taken Reba's life, having spilled her essence, her killer is now bound to her blood.

Or so Simon argued as he imposed his will on reality, twisting it for his own purposes. There would be a price, there always was, but if he planned it right someone else would pay it.

Slowly reality yielded, showing all the connections to the blood in front of him. Reba's family, her loved ones, those regulars who used her time and again, the ones who sold her the drugs that had kept her a slave to the street.

These last two groups Simon marked. They were at least morally responsible for her being in the garage on her last day of life. When tonight's bill came due they would pay part of it.

Finally her last minutes. Simon waited for the moment of her death. Mercifully it came quickly. Then was Reba's her connection to her killer the strongest, and Simon followed this thread to Jack.

He sensed him, he found him. The being that was Jack became aware of him. That's when Simon pushed, dragging them both into a private pocket of reality.

In what appeared to be a darkened alley, with just enough light to see, they faced each other in a place familiar to them both. There was no hiding there. Simon was himself, Sebastian Church, Thomas Defreyne, and others. Jack shifted, changing appearance, the weapon in his hand changing from butcher's knife to doctor's scalpel to a military dagger to a barber's razor.

"So that's how you did it," Simon said, more calmly than he felt. The thought of Weston Ellis came to mind, only there was no Fel to ram her fist through this one's back. Not that that would have worked where he and Jack were. "You rode them, a different body for each murder."

"And now I'm riding the psychic," Jack replied, his voice changing as he did. "And there's naught you can do about it. She's an innocent. Kill her and there's a stain on your soul you can't wash off. Me, I'll just find another host."

Simon wasted no further time in banter. He launched a mental blast at Jack, bringing the killer to his knees. Smiling, Jack came up quickly, knife in one hand, razor in the other. But this was Simon's little piece of existence. He easily sidestepped the Ripper then grabbed him from behind and smashed him into a wall that hadn't been a second ago.

Jack spit out blood. "Having fun, are we? We both know this don't mean beans. Kill me, chop me into little pieces," Jack threw a meat cleaver at Simon's feet. "Use this to do it if you like. But none of it goes back to the real world."

"Look around you, Jack, back in that world. Feel around you. There's a demon from the Pit on your trail. And she has no problem taking down Miss Brooks. And when she's done with her, she'll take that shriveled piece of rancid fat you call a soul and drag you back where you came from."

Jack paused, his attention split between the two planes of reality. When he came back Simon could tell he had located Fel and recognized her nature, or thought he did.

"What do you want?"

"We meet in the garage where you killed your Catherine Eddowes. We work something out."

"What about the police and that demon?"

"It's my show. The police are just the audience. As for the demon, she does what I tell her. And I give you my word that neither she nor I will take any action against you."

Sensing that Simon spoke the truth, the killer who called himself "Jack" asked, "Why?"

"We, meaning me and the police, want you out of Baltimore. This is my city and I can't have your kind going around killing people. The police will find someone to blame the murders on and pretend you didn't happen."

"I get one more kill, have to collect the set. What's one more dead whore?"

Simon shook his head. "She's getting closer to you, Jack. When she gets to you, it's back to the Pit, this time a few circles further down. They don't like escapees. Find your Mary Kelly somewhere else."

Simon sensed the killer's agreement. "Don't keep me waiting," he said, then returned to his body.

"Simon, are you okay?"

"Fine, or I will be if all goes well. Now then, please, will you step away from this? For there is truly no turning back."

"I wish I could, Simon."

The Question was asked, the Choice made. Simon could only reply, "So do I, Caitlin Robin Hood." As her eyes widened in surprise, he added with a smile. "What, did you think I wouldn't find out?"

The sergeant's radio crackled. She gave it a "10-4" and said, "Your 60-year woman is here." Another crackle. "And Fel is right behind her."

"Last chance to stay in the Garden, Katie."

Detective hood shook her head.

"Then leave your weapon holstered, your mouth shut, and just watch. And hope this works. If it doesn't, well, they'll eventually find us in the rubble after this garage collapses around us."

The body of Josephine Brooks walked into the garage. Despite the weather, it was wearing an overcoat from which it drew a large and very sharp knife. Behind him, Simon imagined Caitlin's hand twitching as she fought against drawing her pistol. Behind Jack was Fel, guarding the entrance to the garage, ready to stop the killer from escaping whatever the cost to her.

"Right on time, Jack."

"About our deal …"

"First things first. Is that the knife you used here and in the other cities?" The killer nodded Brooks's head. "We'll need it, to plant on our patsy." At Jack's hesitation, Simon said, "You can find another Precious, give us the knife and you and I are done."

A clatter as the metal blade hit concrete. "I'll be going then."

"Yes, you will," Simon said coldly. "He's yours."

A laugh that chilled the souls of all filled the air. Fel heard it, knew it of old, and almost ran. But she stood her ground and stayed at her post. She had changed, and the thing that appeared in the shadows with dark, red eyes and very sharp teeth no longer had a claim on her.

Jack also knew what it was. "You lied," he yelled at Simon and prepared to flee. But Simon was in front of him and when he turned, there was Fel. And his knife was on the ground.

"I only said that neither I nor Fel nor the police would take any action against you." The Pit creature that was dragging the shadows with it moved towards Jack. Simon said again, "He's yours," then added, "but only him. Leave the woman."

"And how will you stop me?" the shadow form asked, its voice like nails on a slate.

"He won't. I will."

There appeared before them a being in the shape of a woman. No longer looking plain, her hair was a nimbus around her. She was all in white, her robes banishing all shadows but the one she had addressed. Her feet were bare and still did not touch the ground.

This time Fel had the urge to run toward this creature, but again she stayed where she was. She had not changed enough and did not feel worthy.

In a voice like a song, the Messenger said, "Take what is yours, and only that, and return you both to the Pit. Do not make me shine the Light in your direction."

An inky tentacle reached toward the body of Josephine Brooks, touched it gently. There was wail of pain that came from the Ripper's soul as it was sucked back into the shadows of Hell, its punishment to be long and painful, one that would become a legend in the depths of Hell and a warning to all those would defy its masters.

The shadow shrank, the eyes fading away, leaving only the toothsome smile. And before that faded, it said to Simon, "Such awaits you on your next visit."

The mage smiled in reply. "I'll cross that bridge when I come to it, and whenever I want."

Simon then turned towards the shining Light. As he had sometime before, he resisted the urge to kneel before it.

Before anyone else could speak, Miss Brooks cried out and collapsed on the ground. Simon ran to her, gave her some of his strength, and helped her stand.

"Oh, thank you," Miss Brooks said, hugging Simon. "He, it was inside me and made me do terrible things, horrible things. And he made me watch. And then I'd forget, until the next time, and I'd remember it all. But now he's gone, and, and … Oh God, I still remember!"

She would have fallen again, had Simon not been holding her. The Messenger moved toward her, but Simon waved her back.

"No, it's up to her. Free will and all that. One of Their better ideas. To Miss Brooks he said, "Josephine, listen to me. If you want we can make you forget what he did, what he made you do. Or you can choose to remember. Either way, now that you know what could happen, if it happens again you will be held responsible. Do you understand?'

"Yes, I think so."

"Know so. If you take the chance and fail, that shadow will come for you. Or we can make it so it will never happen again. Do you understand that?"

It took a moment but she finally did. "I won't be special anymore."

Simon was about say something like, "We are all special," even knowing that it would not help, when the Messenger said,

"Right now there are unborn in need of a soul. You could start over."

Without hesitating, Miss Brooks said, "I think I'd like that."

The Question having been asked, the Choice having been made, a bright Light flew toward the Messenger who took it to herself even as the body of Josephine Brooks again collapsed, this time never to rise.

Her work done, Simon expected the Messenger to fade away, but instead, she turned toward Fel and said, "Stay on the path, Sister." Only then did she leave.

The danger gone, The Powers Above and Below satisfied, the body of the killer on the ground next to the weapon that had been used in multiple murders across four cities, Simon turned toward Caitlin to ask how she was going to explain yet another heart attack. But the detective looked stunned, her face tanned from exposure to the Light and her soul in turmoil at the Truth she had just witnessed.

"Fel, take Caitlin home, comfort her however you must. I'll call Timothy Payne and work things out with him."

Simon then spoke softly to Caitlin. "The Knowledge of Good and Evil. They truly exist, Katie, there really is a Heaven and Hell. It's a heavy burden, but one I'm sure you're strong enough to bear. Now go with Fel and let her take care of you."

The Price of Eternal Youth

The fantasy convention known as the Tir na Con was similar to most conventions of its kind. It had panels on art, writing, and what was believed to be the life, loves, and practices of the Fae. It had demonstrations on how to make elf ears and fairy wings and workable mermaid tails. It also has an extensive dealers' room, which sold books, jewelry, costumes, and other items designed to separate the convention goers from their money.

What made Tir na Con different from the other conventions was that in its second year it attracted the attention of a paladin in service to the Lady of the Plant Annwn, which lies somewhere in the east of the Land of the Afternoon. His quest complete, he visited that which had a name that was both familiar and different. And he brought back word of the gathering to the land known by mortals as Fairie.

Ever since then, beings from that land, who called themselves the Gentry, under Articles of Truce and wearing glamours that disguised their true natures, visited this convention to enjoy what was a celebration of themselves and their life.

Ginny London was the owner of London Books and longtime vendor at Tir na Con. Having the Sight, she was also one of the first to see the otherworldly visitors for who they really were. So when a conflict developed between members of the Unseelie Court and the Plant Annwn that threatened to not only break the Truce but to destroy a good bit of Hunt Valley, Maryland, it was she who called in her friend Simon Tombs to broker the peace, after he had broken a few bones of course.

Time passed, too fast for Ginny. When the convention moved to the Hotel Albion on the Bay, on the shores of the Chesapeake, her age prevented her from attending. But since Simon always attended anyway, he graciously agreed to work the London's Books table for her.

It was the Thursday before the convention. Simon and his mostly reformed demon companion Fel had spent the day setting up Ginny's booth then stocking it with books that were selected to appeal to customers both human and otherwise.

Their work done for the day, Simon covered the shelves with magic cloths designed to prevent peeking, pilfering, and outright theft then he and Fel retired to their rooms.

It was nearing evening, the time for which Simon had been waiting. Fel was in the bathroom. On hearing the thunder, Simon Tombs looked out the window of his bayfront room. His room was on the top floor so his view of the bay was one of the best. And whenever possible, Simon preferred the best.

"Fel," he called to his companion, "come see this."

"I'm in the bathroom," Fel called back.

"Well, unless you're doing something that should not be interrupted, come here."

Fel came out of the bathroom wearing only panties and a perturbed look. She had spent most of the day hauling and stacking books. She was tired, sweaty, and needed a shower. Showers and baths were luxuries that had been not available to her in the Pit from which Simon had summoned her and she enjoyed them almost as much as she enjoyed other pleasures of the flesh such as sleep, sex, mint chocolate chip ice cream, and the alcoholic mixture known as a Pepper Special.

"What is it, Simon?"

Simon turned at her question. The sight of Fell standing there in almost nothing distracted him from the view out of the window. But only for a moment.

"Look to the north," he said.

Fel did and saw lightning open a rift above the waters of the Chesapeake Bay. Through this rift, heralded by thunder, sailed three ships. The first to come through was dark-hulled and bore golden sails. The next was built of a lighter wood, its sails scarlet. The third ship was white and silver. It has no sails and no oars, but still moved gracefully through the water.

The Gentry had arrived.

"You do realize, Simon, that the Lords of the Pit and the Fair Folk have been at war since the Second Rebellion?"

He nodded. "Yes, I do. The Unseelie Court at first sided with the Morningstar, only to betray him when Plant Annwn and the Tuatha de Danann threatened to join with the Host. The Betrayer did not like being betrayed. But I wouldn't worry, Fel. You are less than you were, and more. You are by your own making a Guardian and I will make it clear that you are under my protection."

The evening before a con is always a strange one. The Albion was quiet, as if waiting for the next day's onslaught. The fifty or so members of the Gentry mostly stayed in their rooms, coming down only to eat and look around. A select few found their way to the bar, which called itself The Grail. Once they were gathered, Simon and Fel joined them, Simon in a suit, Fel in a modest blue dress.

"My Lords and Ladies of the Fae," he said, addressing them. "May I present my companion, the Lady Fel, Guardian Demon of Baltimore."

Simon's revelation of Fel's nature caused some excitement among the Gentry. Before they could react, however, he went on.

"The Lady Fel is under my protection. I will not vouch for her good behavior. There is no need. Her behavior this weekend will speak for itself. If there are any objections, let them be raised now. If there be any challenges, let them be made now."

In her association with Simon Tombs, Fel had often heard him speak with threat and menace, but on that day Simon was not speaking to mortals but to beings of power. Yet the sound of his voice, the look in his eyes, and the smile on his lips told her, and them, that he was equal to their power and would oppose them if he must.

For her.

Not for the first time did the once demon of the Pit feel a warmth for the one who had drawn her from it, the one who treated her as a friend and partner rather than the slave she could have been. And she wondered how she could have ever believed that she would betray him.

Although they had cloaked themselves in glamour to appear as human, Fel saw the true nature of the ones at the table. From their dress, they seemed to be noble born. One of them stood.

"Lord Mage, on behalf of all here, I will confess that your companion was somewhat of a surprise to us. Yet if she is with you she cannot be against us. So," and here he bowed towards Fel, "although we are guests here, I bid you welcome, Lady Fel. May there be peace and joy between us."

Fel returned the bow and said, "Thank you, Sir."

"Yes, thank you, Prince Victor. Fel, Prince Victor and Lady Deidre are of the Plant Annwn. May I also present Duke Mikel and Lady Saber of the Unseelie Court, and Queen Donagh and King Finarra of the Tuatha de Danann. And now, we are in a tavern, and none of us must rise early in the morning, so why are we wasting time talking?"

It was some hours later that Fel and Simon made their way back to their room, each of them having declined invitations to join certain members of the Gentry in theirs. On the elevator, Fel asked, "Lord Mage?"

"It was that or Sorcerer Supreme, and that doctor fellow took that title."

It was the first day of the convention and Simon and Fel were ready. Simon Tombs was dressed as the mage he was. His magician's robes were one part Jedi master, another part Gandalf, and a third of his own design. He liked wearing robes and sometimes wished he dared wear them in public, for they hid so much more than mundane clothing.

Since Simon was the master magician, Fel was dressed as his apprentice. The clothes Simon had chosen for her were dark trousers, a white shirt, and a vest to match her pants, the kind of clothing he imagined a male apprentice might wear. In spite of this, or maybe because of it, her costume only enhanced Fel's feminine beauty and appearance without going to the extremes some of the other attendees, of all genders, dared.

Twenty minutes before the opening, Simon and Fel removed

the magic cloths from their wares and when the cry of "Tir na Con has begun. The Dealers' Room is now open" came they settled in for what they hoped would be a busy weekend of selling books and a quiet one with regard to everything else.

The rest of the day went as it had in the past, the true humans walking around, checking out the tables, promising to return later in the weekend, Simon resisting the urge to cast small compulsions to make them keep their promise. The disguised Gentry, however, bought what they wanted as soon as they saw it. At the London's Books table, they proved partial to westerns, romances, and crime novels.

During a slow period, Simon sent Fel off to look around the dealers' room. She came back with a black cloak, a red corset, a nasty looking dagger, and a pair of wings. When she showed Simon the latter, she said sadly, "I used to have a real pair."

Hugging her, he replied, "And I'm sure you will again."

Later it was his turn. There were other book dealers there, and Simon added to his personal collection. He bought a necklace to match Fel's new corset and a new leather belt. He also picked up a specially crafted wand (a wizard cannot have too many wands) he had ordered the previous year.

Simon examined the wand "Very nice, a fine piece of work."

"It's a little heavy," the wand master said, "because of the special insert. I never done one like that before. These days most people want peacock feathers or something, because of that boy wizard. Still, I can't knock the movies or books. They're great for business."

After paying for the wand, Simon was on his way back to Fel when he noticed the face-painting booth. Running the booth was an attractive woman closer to thirty than twenty. She was clothed in a simple white dress. The dress was cut just enough to hint at her ample charms and from the way she moved Simon would have bet his new wand that those charms were unrestrained.

The woman was turning a boy into a tiger. He was young enough not to take notice of how much she wasn't dressed. Behind her were examples of her work. For the kids, there were movie, comic, and cartoon characters. For teens and adults, there was a selection of intricate geometric patterns. There was also a privacy screen in the back of the booth for those who wanted some place other than their face painted.

Something was pulling Simon towards the booth. It was not only the attractive woman. There was something about some of her designs, something that was not quite right, something that threatened to bring back old and best-forgotten memories. He shook the feeling off and returned to his table.

Where Fel was talking to what appeared to be a potential customer. She did not look happy with the man. When Simon got closer he heard,

"No, honey, you don't understand. I'm not interested in any of these old books, I'm interested in the bookseller. How about after the room closes you and I go up my room and get it on?"

Fel declined but the man persisted, not seeming to understand the word "No."

Don't make her angry, Simon thought. *You wouldn't like her when she's angry.*

Simon used his Sight. There was no glamour so he was not Gentry, just a boorish, human oaf. Simon held back to see how Fel would handle him.

Handle him she did, saying, "Well, you do make me hot." With that, she reached out and grabbed his wrist. A bit of her demonic nature came through and there was a slight sizzle and a faint odor of burnt flesh. The oaf pulled away.

"What the …"

"Let's go to your room, right now," Fel said with feigned enthusiasm. "I can't wait to get my hands on the rest of you, especially your …"

The oaf disappeared. The burn mark on his wrist never did.

Simon rejoined Fel with a "Well done, Apprentice."

"Thank you, *Master*." Then after a moment's thought asked, "Just what does a sorcerer's apprentice do?"

"She takes care of her master's needs."

"You mean like polishing your wand?"

"Later, when you've cooled down."

The dealers' room closed at seven. The plan was for Simon and Fel to have dinner then to further explore the duties of a Sorcerer's Apprentice. Unlike most of Simon's plans, this one did not go smoothly.

As they were putting the magic cloths over the books, a member of the Gentry came up. "Lord Mage, forgive this interruption, but your presence is requested on the fourteenth floor."

The fourteenth floor was the one reserved for the Gentry. *This cannot be good*, Simon thought. Turning to Fel he said, "Go have dinner, attend some panels, I may be a while."

"I think I'll just go up to my room and rest for when you get back." She gave him a smile that suggested he might get no rest that night.

She may not betray me, but she just might kill me anyway, Simon said to himself. *Well, in that case, I won't mind dying.*

"And you are?" Simon asked the fae who had come to get him.

"Forgive me, Lord Mage. I am Fredag, and serve the Lady as a guardsman."

"The lady of which court?"

"My lord, I serve *The* Lady, the One who rules over all. She who brought us peace."

"I understand." And Simon did. The Lady was at the top of the Gentry's pantheon, according to some. There were those who served darker gods, or none at all.

When they arrived on the fourteenth floor, Fredag led Simon to a room in which were the rulers of the three courts, along with as many of the Gentry as would fit. On the two double beds lay three fae, one in one bed, two in the other. At first glance Simon thought them asleep, but then he noticed that their naturally pale complexions were almost white, and their breathing was very shallow, maybe one or two breaths a minute.

"They were found on the floors of their rooms, Lord Mage," the Lady Deidre explained. They were brought in here where Finchbeard," she indicated an Unseelie male standing between the beds, "cast a life-sustaining spell."

"Which will do little good," the Fae healer said in a gruff voice. "Their spirits have fled."

"Can you help us, Lord Mage?" asked a worried Prince Victor. Two of the stricken were of the Plant Annwn, the other was an Unseelie.

Simon thought about Fel waiting for him and the promise of her smile. *There goes my evening. Well, at least I'll live another day.* Then he looked at the assembled Gentry, most of whom were not looking back kindly. *Maybe.*

Something nagged at him, something he'd seen, an old memory. But before he could explore that thought or offer whatever help he could there came a voice from the side.

"Why ask him?"

"Nilus, be still," ordered Duke Mikel.

"Forgive me, my Duke, but I cannot. It's clear to all that this is the work of that Pit scum he keeps as a pet. She's stolen their spirits and sent them to her true masters. But not to worry, I've taken care of her."

Damn. Simon was not often at a loss as to what to do, but this was one of those times. Help the three stricken, go to Fel, or teach Nilus and who knew how many more an extreme lesson in manners.

Before he could decide, *Devil with a Blue Dress On* sounded from the phone in his robe. Fel. He breathed one sigh of relief and another of worry, then said to the assembled Gentry, "Forgive me, but I have to take this."

"Fel, what happened?"

"Simon, there's a whimpering elf curled up our room." On hearing this, he put the phone on speaker.

"Why is he whimpering?"

"I hit him."

"With what?"

"My foot."

"Where?"

"Where do you think?'

"That would explain the whimpering. Where there any others?"

"Just one. He's scorched and unconscious."

"Hold on." He addressed Mikel. "Sir Duke, can your kind survive a fall from a great height?"

Duke Mikel was not a happy Fae. Not only did one of his court act without his approval, two others had been easily defeated by what appeared to be, demon or not, a young girl. He and his court had been shamed. Amends must be made and punishment meted out. The last was easy.

"I suppose we'll find out."

Simon nodded his thanks then said into the phone. "Fel, throw them out the window. Try to hit the pool, but don't try too hard."

"Lord Mage, for the actions of my court ..."

Simon cut him off. "Say nothing, my lord Duke. There is no blame on you or yours unless you wish it so. Otherwise, this is between me and," Simon looked at the one who had sent his friends, "Nilus, is it?"

Nilus looked at Mikel. "My duke?"

Mikel said, "You acted alone, you stand alone." He then turned his back on his retainer.

Before Nilus could react to what he perceived as a betrayal, Simon said, "Nilus, I told you last night that the Lady Fel was under my protection. Your attack on her was an attack on me. Still, no harm was done except to your friends. For the respect I have for all others here present, in the interest of peace between my world and yours, I'm inclined to be merciful. Apologize to me, and later to the Lady Fel, and I will be satisfied."

It was a generous offer. The Choice had been given, all awaited Nilus's reply.

The Answer was short, just two words, and physically impossible except for two of those present.

Too bad, Simon thought as he took his newly purchased wand from his robes.

Nilus laughed. "That magic stick won't help you. In this world, we are magic."

"I know."

Simon knew many spells, curses, and enchantments. He used none of them. Instead, he hit Nilus with a blast of pure energy, fueled by his will and powered by the core of cold iron within his new wand.

Giving out a cry of anguish, Nilus collapsed. At his Duke's nod, Finchbeard rushed over to him. "He's alive but unconscious."

Simon addressed Mikel, "And he will remain so until his return to Fairie. Should he ever return to this plane, it is here he will die."

Duke Mikel nodded, as did many of the others. "A fair and imaginative solution, Lord Mage. I only wish you could do something for our stricken comrades."

"As do I. But I'm sure Finchbeard and the other healers present have done what they could. Let them treat the symptoms while we search for the cause."

"We?" asked Lady Saber.

"We." Simon turned toward Fredag. "How many guardsmen are present?"

"Three, one per court. Myself, Guardsman Bran, and Guardswoman Patrice, all serving the Lady's Justice."

Simon indicated the three on the bed. "Then trace their movements, from when they arrived to when they were found. Where they went, what they ate, what they bought, and to whom they spoke. A common answer may lead to a solution."

Simo then took his leave. Once in the hallway …

"Lord Mage?"

"Yes, Fredag."

"Take care. Not all are convinced that you or you … companion are not to blame. And a core of iron cannot stop a knife in the back or a bolt from afar."

Simon smiled. "Very astute, Guardsman. When this is over we will have to drink deep and tell tall tales."

"Looking forward to it, Lord Mage."

"To you, Fredag, it's Simon."

When he returned to his room, Simon found Fel in the mood righteous violence usually caused. Neither of them went to bed early and when they did, they did not fall asleep until another hour had passed. When he finally woke up, Simon wondered in how many other rooms such activities had taken place. How many demi-Fae would be born on the other side of the rift? How many mortal children would develop special abilities … such as magic? He put that last thought far from his mind, gulped breakfast, aroused, or rather, awakened Fel and went to the Dealers' Room to face Saturday at Tir na Con.

As he walked down the many flights of stairs – the elevators were too crowded and gravity did most of the work – his thoughts turned to the stricken Gentry. He did not remember seeing them on Friday, but the Gentry tended to change glamours according to their moods. Whatever it was, he hoped that the Guardsmen would find the common link.

The Guardian of the Gate to the Dealers' Room was in a puckish mood that morning. "Stop," she said. "To proceed further you must answer a riddle. What is it that a man does standing up, a woman does sitting down, and a dog does on three legs?"

Simon was likewise feeling puckish. He looked at the young woman and said, "42," a good answer but not the right one. Before the guardian could say so, Simon added, "You said I had to answer. You did not say I had to answer correctly."

She smiled and let him pass.

That bit of wordplay, coupled with his night with Fel, had Simon in a good mood. This mood vanished when he walked entered the dealer's room proper. Jewelry, costumes, masks, face painting, wands, wings, books …

Simon stopped. Like the day before, something teased his mind. He walked back to the face painting booth.

The woman running the booth was the same as the night before. The dress she was wearing was just as alluring, hinting at her body but not revealing it, actually modest for a young woman at an event like this.

Young woman? Simon thought. She had not appeared young the night before. Old memories again fought to surface and did so with a mental shudder or two. Simon found himself staring, not at the woman but at her designs.

Most were for the kids. But others were more elaborate, abstract with touches of Celtic, Norman, Old Roman, and Slavic. Some were so intricate one could lose oneself in their patterns.

Or lose one's self.

"Interested in a henna tattoo, good sir?"

"Not for me," Simon said. "But maybe I'll send my girlfriend over later. How much are they?"

The young woman, whose com badge identified her as "Veil" shook her head. "No charge, but donations to the cause are always welcome." She pointed to a glass jar labeled "Offerings."

"Free?" Simon asked, as if amazed that anything was free at a con. "For any of these?"

"You girlfriend is free to choose any she likes." Veil pointedly looked at the privacy screen. "Anywhere she likes."

A choice freely made, an offering freely given. The memory came back. He had been Sebastian then, and the police had called him in on what was being called the Husk Plague. It was, he determined, occult in origin but the source and the cause were long gone. A magical time bomb.

He risked the Sight, hoping that woman before him could not detect its use. Three of the designs turned red. Not good. Two turned black. Even worse.

Smiling at Veil, Simon thanked her and said that his girlfriend would be by later that day.

"You promise?"

"You can be sure of it."

When he got to the London's Books table, she saw Fel with three potential customers. He watched as she sold them each something. *She's good at this*, he thought, then reasoned, *and why not? She still has some demon in her. And demons are good at finding what people want and making deals so they get it.*

"Fel," he told her once the customers had left. "I'll need you to work the table alone for a while, maybe most of the day. Something from last night just came up."

As soon as he said he was sorry he did. After Fel's "And you call me insatiable" he explained, "No the other matter. With our guests."

"Oh, how can I help?"

"Work the table, sell the books. Right now I have to figure out how to keep more of the Gentry from being stricken and how to prevent them from tearing my suspect apart. Then I have to figure out how many humans may have been infected and how to cure them."

He left the Dealers' Room thinking about his problems. By the time the elevator doors had opened he had solved two of them. He had the third figured out by the time he arrived on the fourteenth floor.

Simon entered the room where the three stricken Gentry lay. They were now lying face down, with Guardsmen Brad, Patrice, and Fredag examining them under the supervision of Finchbeard. One of the fae had a tramp stamp just above her buttocks. The other two had henna tattoos on their backs. All three designs were among those that had turned red or black when Simon had Viewed them downstairs.

"We found the common thread, Lord Simon. All three had their bodies painted by that woman in white downstairs."

As Fredag said this, he and he fellow guardsmen exchanged worried looks. Simon guessed why but didn't say.

"She's the cause." He gave them a brief explanation. "The spell is meant for humans. It worked differently on your kind, stealing their life forces now instead of later."

"More than these three were painted, Lord Mage," Finchbeard said. "Shall I expect more patients?"

Instead of replying to the Healer, Simon turned to the guardsmen. "Let's see them."

Reluctantly Fredag and Brad exposed their left arms to show matching Tinker Bells drawn there. Simon looked at Patrice who asked, "Mine's on my left breast. Must I?"

Although tempted, he shook his head. "I'm sure it looks very lovely there." To all three he said, "You're safe, as I'm sure the others are as well. Only certain designs were cursed."

There was a general sigh of relief. Then Fredag asked, "What do we do now?"

"That bitch is dead," Brad replied simply.

"Yes, she is," Simon agreed. "Soon but not right away. And for now, this stays with the five of us. If the others find out …"

"There goes the Articles of Truce."

"Exactly. Now, then, are there any artists among you that can do that kind of work?" Simon indicated the designs on the stricken fae.

"I can," Brad said. "I was an artist before I became a guardsman. I still practice the art."

Simon smiled. "Good. Now here's what we're going to do. Guardsman Brad, you're going to hate this plan."

Guardsman Brad approached Veil's booth

"Back again?" Veil asked.

Brad nodded. "I'd like another one," he said. He pointed to a unicorn. "That one."

"Good choice. Where would you like it?"

"We'll … have to go behind the screen," Brad answered, doing his best to look embarrassed. Which he was, but not for the reason the woman thought.

Minutes went by, then …

"Someone help." Veil ran out from behind the privacy screen. "He's fainted." Fredag and Patrice rushed toward the booth. Going behind the screen, Fredag got the groggy Brad to his feet.

"He'll be okay," Fredag announced to all those listening, "He has these spells. We'll just take him up to his room."

In the excitement, no one noticed Patrice remove the samples of the five designs that Simon had indicated. Veil took her place in the booth, apparently not noticing that the designs were missing.

All was not what it had seemed. As soon Veil had followed Brad behind the screen she was startled by him turning into her. Before she could react, he struck her hard in the face, knocking her down and out. He then cast a secondary glamour so that anyone seeing the true Veil would see only the human version of Brad.

For the rest of the day, Brad in the image of Veil worked the booth, painted faces and other body parts, and fended off improper advances and suggestions from several men and two women. *The mage was right, I do not like this*, he thought. But he was a guardsman and pledged to do his duty no matter what. So he soldiered on and resolved to change his own ways of approaching women.

On the fourteenth floor, in a room separate from the one where the stricken lay, the unconscious body of the woman who called herself Veil was tied to a chair. Brad's glamour was off and she had been stripped to her panties.

"Is that necessary?" Queen Donagh had asked when Simon had given that order.

"Yes, Your Highness. You will soon see why. Is the artist here?"

A fae named Tempest stepped forward. "I am here, Lord Mage," she said.

"Good. Paint these on her body. Back, both arms, both legs. Be sure to recreate them exactly."

"I shall."

As Tempest worked, Simon turned to face the others in the room. They included Fredag and Patrice, the rulers of the three courts, and several of the court nobles. Before he could speak, Prince Victor asked,

"Will the Lady Fel be joining us?"

Simon shook his head. "What I am about to attempt is dark magic. Even practiced for a good and noble cause it can stain one's soul. The Lady Fel is working towards redemption. It is a hard road she travels and I would not have that journey impaired."

He paused, then continued. "I need only one from each court, to serve as witnesses. All others may be excused. Any who stay may share the cost of what I am about to do."

Despite Simon's warning, none left the room. He bowed to them. "The honor and bravery of the Gentry is proven this day."

Tempest had finished her work. Simon inspected it and found no flaws.

"Thank you, Lady Tempest. You may leave if you wish."

"I stand with the rest."

"Good for you."

Taking an ashwood wand from his robe (Simon didn't need it,

but he did like to put on a show) he gestured and said, "Awaken." Veil stirred, woke up, and started struggling against her bonds.

"What the … Untie me, you bastards. How dare you …"

It was then that Veil looked about her. The Gentry had dropped their glamours and Veil soon realized that she was in a room filled with beings not quite human. Fear replaced anger on her face.

Simon addressed her. "You who are called Veil. I sense within you three spirits that are not yours. Further, you have within you ties to souls that were not yours to claim. I ask you now, will you willingly relinquish those souls and spirits?"

"Go to Hell."

"Been there, done that, saved some souls, forgot the T-shirt. I ask you again, will you willingly relinquish those souls and spirits to which you have laid claim?"

"My master will have you, Tombs, and you will suffer in the Pit for all time."

"Many have tried. They are still in Hell, and I am not. I ask a third time, will you willingly relinquish those souls and spirits to which you have laid claim?"

Veil's answer was to curse Simon, spewing the vilest epithets he had ever heard, some in languages that had not been spoked in hundreds of years.

Three times the Choice had been offered. Three times the Answer had been given. With no other alternative, Simon sighed and said carefully chosen words.

"Droim ar ais. Scaoileadh."

(Reverse. Release.)

The woman who called herself Veil screamed. She continued to scream as the designs painted on her body glowed a sickly green and began to burn their way into her. She screamed as the souls and spirits she had captured were pulled one by one from her body. And once these had been freed, the spell that Simon had prepared and cast continued to work, stripping the woman of all the life forces she had stolen over many years and returning them to the Source from where they came. Soon all her stolen youth was gone and she began to age. Hours, days, weeks, months, and years left her, and still she screamed until she was too weak to do more than whimper. And when she could not even do that what was left of her body crumbled into dust, and then even that was gone.

It was over.

One by one, the Gentry left the room, their rulers the last to leave but one. Simon remained and briefly considered what he had done.

That last day the books sold well, most of the purchases made by grateful members of the Gentry. Brad, having changed his glamour to as close to his true self as a human could get, was having such a good time at the face-painting booth that only the threat of being left behind caused him to leave it. The three formerly stricken fae stopped by bowed to Simon.

"We were trapped inside her," said one.

"You saved us," said another.

"If you ever need us, you have only to call," said the third.

Soon there came the cry of "The Dealer's Room is now closed. The Tir na Con has ended. Good night, and joy be to you all."

Simon and Fel had their room for one more night. And so it was that as evening came on the last day, they watched from the window as three ships sailed north through a rift above the waters of the Chesapeake Bay and the Gentry returned to Fairie.

Once they were gone, Fel asked, "Simon, what happened last night?"

"Best you don't know. But it's over."

Simon Tombs was not often wrong. But on that day, he was.

Story's End

When the woman last known as "Veil" regained awareness she found herself in the same state she was in when she died – tied to a chair and stripped to her panties, with Hellish designs on her arms, legs, and back. She remembered dying, the pain of her demise still fresh in her mind. She remembered who had killed her – Simon Tombs, a mage who had too often taken the side of the Divine thus earning the enmity of the Pit. And she remembered why she had died.

"Did you succeed?" Multiple voices each with their own high-pitched squeal, each a sharp needle through her head.

"Yes," she managed to say. "When I cursed him I slipped in the words you told me to say."

"Good. Well done, our loyal servant. Your sacrifice pleases us."

Veil breathed a sigh of relief. Long had she sacrificed unwitting humans to her dark masters, tricking her victims into choosing their own destruction, destruction that was delayed so that she was elsewhere when it occurred. For hundreds of years she had done this, retaining her youth and beauty in exchange for the deaths of others, knowing that one day the remainder of the price would come due.

That day was shortly before the Tir na Con, when fairies walked among humans. The Pit Lords had come to her then, told her what she must do.

"There will be no delay with the accursed Gentry," the voices told her. "Their spirits will be taken at once. Tombs will suspect you, then he will take you, and he will have to kill you to reverse the spell. Before he does, you will mark him for us."

They told her how, what words to say, and how to hide them.

"And why should I do this?"

The shadows that surrounded her grew darker and deeper, the toothsome smiles appearing sharper.

"Do this and you will be among the chosen of Perdition. Slaves will attend to your every need, and you will feast on the flesh of angels and saints. Refuse us, fail us, and it is you who will be the slave, and others will feast on you."

Veil made her Choice, lured the hated Simon Tombs into her trap, and planted the seeds of his destruction within him.

And now on a plane of Hell, one that was bordered by a wide chasm over which a bridge sometimes appeared, the woman last known as Veil dared to ask,

"I have done all that you asked. Now I ask for my reward."

Her answer was mocking, hellish laughter that hurt her more than the squealing voices had. "There is no reward in the Pit. There is only betrayal and pain for those foolish enough to believe us. In serving us, you have earned this."

A mighty wind, carrying with it the stench of a dozen slaughterhouses, came up and blew her, chair and all, into the chasm. And the woman fell. And as she fell, the demonic designs on her body again burned their way into her. And she knew that they would burn for as long as she fell and that she would fall for a long, long time. But not forever. Forever would come after she stopped falling, for then true pain would be hers.

But as she fell, the woman Veil lashed out at her masters' betrayal with one of her own. Using the power of the symbols on her body, symbols with which she had worked for hundreds of years, she sent one word to him who, by killing her, had created a bond with her.

"Beware!"

Then all she knew was falling and pain.

Every contact leaves a trace.

It is one of the first things crime scene investigators learn, for the principle of "There is no contact without transfer" is the basis of what they do. It is also the basis for several different kinds of magic, many of which were practiced by Simon Tombs.

It would have been good if Simon had remembered this. That whatever he touched when employing his talents also touched him, leaving their marks.

When he used a deadly spell to reverse the one cast by Veil on the guests at the Tir na Con, he created a bond between the two of them. That Veil had marked him with carefully chosen words only strengthened this bond.

When Simon created a bridge to Perdition and repeatedly use dthis bridge to release repentant souls from punishment, he failed to realize that bridges go both ways, and what being could build another could use, and what was torn down could be rebuilt.

And Fel – Simon's companion, lover, friend, and partner – was herself a creature from and of Hell, no matter how far along she was on the road to redemption. She was, as he had been repeatedly warned by her and others, destined to betray him. However unwittingly and unknowingly, she was a scorpion who could not help but sting him.

Any one of these factors would not have been enough. But taken as a whole …

It was early evening, about nine. Simon and Fel were in sitting in their living room binge-watching, again, *Steam Powered Love*. They were just at the point where Dr. Ginderhoff was asking himself "What would James T. Kirk do?" when …

"Beware."

Simon instantly recognized the voice. He then realized the source of the warning and knew he had only seconds, if that long, to act.

"Fel, they're coming."

They had prepared for this day. It did not matter that neither knew just who "they" were, just that the two of them were about to be attacked by malevolent forces. Simon drew on his magics, readied his spells, and strengthened his apartment's wards. Fel looked into her own being, drawing out the growing light within her and hoping that it would be strong enough to defeat the darkness within and without.

The attack when it came was well planned and better executed. Every bit of darkness that was in the apartment turned against them. And where there was no darkness, shadows grew, shadows with red eyes, sharp teeth, and appetites for soul-stealing magicians and traitors to the Pit.

At first, Simon's wards and traps took care of them. Demons appeared and were sent screaming back to Hell, there to suffer the cost of failure. But still more came and the traps filled and the overwhelmed wards began to fail.

Fel called up the light within her. She had named herself "Guardian" and now it was time to earn that name. Every demon, every shadow she faced withered at her glance as she thought back to her time on Assateague Island, when buried memories of Paradise had washed over her. It was these memories that sustained her when her power began to wane and she resorted to ripping the hellish creations apart with her bare hands.

And still the evil things came. For every one that Simon and Fel destroyed, another grew. Simon's apartment was filled with magical artifacts and items of power. He drew strength from these and slaughtered the legions of the Pit as they came one by one, two by two, and three by three.

And still the evil things came. They were the waves of a foul, unending ocean and Simon knew that this time there would be no stopping them. But he smiled and fought on.

"Simon," Fel said, her voice showing panic for the first time since he had known her, "there are too many of them." Still, she punched and ripped and destroyed those with whom she was once allied.

Even as his spells blasted demons and forced back the approaching darkness he understood her fear. She was bound to him, and should he fall, that bond would end. Regardless of the progress she had made towards her redemption, she would be returned to Hell, there to again suffer the punishment imposed on her an eternity ago, a punishment that would only be increased due to her betrayal of her former masters.

Simon could, he knew, take her power for his own. She had once asked him if he could do that. Doing so would no doubt send her to oblivion, as he did not think that her ready to rejoin the

Divine.

There was one thing he could do, however, something that might give her a chance, providing it was only him for whom they had come.

"Felicia Baker," he said, even as the two fought back the ever-growing tide. "You who are known as Fel. As the one who summoned you, as the one who holds power and mastery over you, I release you from any and all obligations to me. I give you leave to walk freely upon the Earth until such time as you are called to your final fate. May you find peace and joy."

It was just the merest of moments of peace amid the chaos of battle as one of the bonds between Fel and Simon snapped. She felt it. For the first time since her Fall, Fel was free. Free to do what she wanted.

But it had possibly come too late. The Pit crawlers were too close. She and Simon were beginning to suffer injuries and it would only be a matter of time before they were overwhelmed.

She knew what she had to do, what she was always meant to do. Pushing aside the shadowy creatures that were almost upon her, she ran. Tearing demons apart as she went, she made it to the apartment door. Opening it, she looked back at Simon and saw what might have been understanding in his eyes. Then she went through it and closed it behind her.

Well, Simon thought, even as he was beset on all sides, *I can't say she didn't warn me.*

When Fel seemingly abandoned Simon to his fate, it was with a purpose. Every contact leaves a trace, like calls to like, this is how Simon had taught her magic. Would that the teacher had heeded his own lesson. Still, his student had listened and remembered. She was of three worlds – now the mortal plane but late of both Hell and Heaven. She needed a place, to be alone to sit and think and to work her own magic.

She found it in the back booth of Sebastian's – Simon's booth. Those who worked there wondered why she had come in alone, as she never had before. At first, they did not approach her, she scared them. But Murphy then remembered that she would always try whatever new drink he'd come up with and so that night he brought her her favorite – a Pepper Special.

Fel nodded thanks, then closed her eyes and, like Simon, pictured a bridge. But this bridge was over a river, one that ran red on one side and clear on the other. She had only to choose a side, then let the current take her where it would.

In the quiet of Sebastian's, Fel asked herself the Question then she made her Choice. In her mind, she stood on one side of the bridge and jumped in. In Sebastian's, no one noticed her slowly fade away, her Pepper Special untouched.

Every religion has its devils and demons and so has methods for banishing them. Simon had made a study of every form of exorcism there was, and had mentally edited and compacted them so that a word or two would result in the entire ritual being enacted. He never dreamed that he would need them all.

The evil things came and were banished by the dozens. But there were dozens more behind them and hundreds behind them. Yet despite their multitudes, despite the injuries they inflicted on him, there were no killing blows.

They don't want me dead, Simon decided, even as he realized that he was being herded towards a certain corner of his living room, a corner where the shadows were the deepest, a corner from which he now heard mocking laughter.

They want me alive, to drag me down into the Pit with them, where they'll keep me alive and suffering until Judgement.

Even as he used the last of his banishing prayers, as he mentally sucked the last bits of magic from what had been his home, Simon knew it was over. There were escapes. Out the front door like Fel. On to the balcony then down to the street. He might survive that, he might not, he'd know when he hit the pavement. But the way had been opened and needed to be closed, otherwise demons would be free to roam the Earth unchecked. There were those who would stop them, but not before they did major damage to his city.

Well, I have fought the good fight and I have run the race. The

Choices I made were my own. Now is the time to keep Faith.

This … is going to hurt.

Up until that moment, Simon had been using the magics around him – his wards, his spells, the objects he had collected. Now he dug deep and summoned the magic within himself, the magic that sustained him, the magic that made him who he was. Still, it would take a minute or two, and Simon prayed that he had even that small amount of time left.

Fel stood before the Gates. They slowly opened and she dropped to her knees as the Three came out. Her head down, she dared not look at Them as she pleaded.

"Please, I will suffer whatever punishment you inflict. I will perform whatever task you set. I will do all that you ask."

"What do you seek that you dare to come here?" asked the First of Them.

She told Them.

"The Cost is high," said the Second.

Fel raised her head. The sight of Them burned her eyes, yet her vision remained.

"I will pay it," she declared, willingly giving up her new found freedom.

There was a pause. It might have been a minute or it could have been a century. However long it took, it was time Fel did not think Simon had. But what was time where she stood?

"When this is over," said the Third, *"you will return to the Pit. That is the Cost. We ask again, will you pay it?"*

No hesitation. "I will."

"There is now a bridge over the Great Chasm between Paradise and Perdition, one that repentant souls may cross. They will need a Guardian to protect them on their journey. Do you accept?'

"For how long?" Fel dared to ask the First.

"Until your penance is complete." replied the Second. *"Until We have forgiven you. Until you have forgiven yourself. We ask again, do you accept?'*

There would be purpose, Fel thought. *That is enough.* Then with a smile she could only have learned from Simon, she said, "I accept."

"*Then*," said the Third, "*you will need this.*" Fire filled her hand. "*And these.*" Her shoulders began to ache, then tear.

"*And you shall not go alone,*" They said together.

And then Fel was gone.

It was almost time. The power within Simon was reaching a critical point. Soon he would no longer be able to contain it. Slowly he let himself be pushed toward the blackness of the portal from where the hellish shadows had emerged. Another half minute and the explosion of his magics would incinerate him, all demons present, and probably render his apartment unfit for resale. It would also close the portal.

The seconds ticked down. The demons pushed harder, forcing him closer and closer towards the black gate of Hell.

You're too late, Simon thought, then smiled and accepted death.

Simon Tombs was not often wrong. But on that day, he was.

Time slowed. Simon felt the magics pushed back into his body as the room grew brighter. Beings of light began to battle with creatures of darkness, dispelling them at a touch.

But then the laughter from the shadows grew louder, and more than demons issued from it. Pit Lords, who until then had been content to watch Simon fight his losing battle, emerged to claim their prize.

The cavalry had come too late. Dark hands reached to grab Simon and pull him down to Hell and he had nothing left with which to stop them except the naming of names.

It was then that the balcony doors were thrown open and a winged being with a fiery sword floated in. Putting herself between Simon and the Pit Lords she thrust and slashed, inflicting the pain of Heaven's Punishment, pain that they would feel in addition to that earned by their many sins. They retreated into the Portal and with Heaven's Mercy, she allowed them to do so. Then her sword flared up and banished all remaining shadows save those caused by her own light.

A weakened Simon collapsed, only to be pulled to his feet by his angelic savior. Being Simon, he dared to look at her. As he said a humble "thank you" her light faded and he saw before him a well-figured natural blonde who appeared to be just shy of twenty.

"Fel?" At her nod, he added, "I should not have doubted you. I'm sorry."

"No, you shouldn't have but you are forgiven." *Even as I am not,* she thought but did not say.

Then Simon noticed the beings of light that had accompanied Fel. "Who are your friends?"

"You saved us, Simon Tombs," said the soul that was once Alan Conrad. "We are only returning the favor." Then he and the other repentant souls Simon had freed from Hell faded away, leaving Simon and Fel alone.

"I told you that you'd get your wings back," he said.

They came at a cost, she thought. *Let him think me redeemed.*

"Must you go?" Simon asked, even knowing the answer.

"Yes, I must, but before I do …"

Light once again filled the apartment, granting it an angel's blessing. Whatever wards Simon had before, they were now renewed and strengthened a hundred-fold.

They walked out on the balcony. There Simon dared to hug an angel who, in turn, wrapped her wings around him in farewell. Then without a word, Fel, former guardian demon of Baltimore, took flight.

Simon watched her as she flew over a four-story hotel that sat between two taller buildings. As she disappeared into the starry blackness he said to himself,

And all this time I thought this was my story.

BIOGRAPHY

JOHN L. FRENCH has worked for over forty years as a crime scene investigator and has seen more than his share of murders, shootings and serious assaults. As a break from the realities of his job, he writes science fiction, pulp, horror, fantasy, and, of course, crime fiction.

In 1992 John began writing stories based on his training and experiences on the streets of Baltimore. His first story "Past Sins" was published in Hardboiled Magazine and was cited as one of the best Hardboiled stories of 1993. More crime fiction followed, appearing in Alfred Hitchcock's Mystery Magazine, the Fading Shadows magazines and in collections by Barnes and Noble. Association with writers like James Chambers and the late, great C.J. Henderson led him to try horror fiction and to a still growing fascination with zombies and other undead things. His first horror story "The Right Solution" appeared in Marietta Publishing's *Lin Carter's Anton Zarnak*. Other horror stories followed in anthologies such as *The Dead Walk* and *Dark Furies*, both published by Die Monster Die books. It was in *Dark Furies* that his character Bianca Jones made her literary debut in "21 Doors," a story based on an old Baltimore legend and a creepy game his daughter used to play with her friends.

John's first book was *The Devil of Harbor City*, a novel done in the old pulp style. *Past Sins* and *Here There Be Monsters* followed. John was also consulting editor for Chelsea House's *Criminal Investigation* series. His other books include *The Assassins' Ball* (written with Patrick Thomas), *Past Sins, Blood Is the Life, The Nightmare Strikes, Monsters Among Us* and *The Last Redhead*. John is the editor of *To Hell in a Fast Car, Mermaids 13*, C. J. Henderson's *Challenge of the Unknown, Camelot 13* (with Patrick Thomas) and (with Greg Schauer) *With Great Power* ...

You can find John on Facebook or you can email him at him at jfrenchfam@ aol.com.

DOWN THESE
MEANS STREETS
of Magic & Monsters walk the

MYSTIC INVESTIGATORS

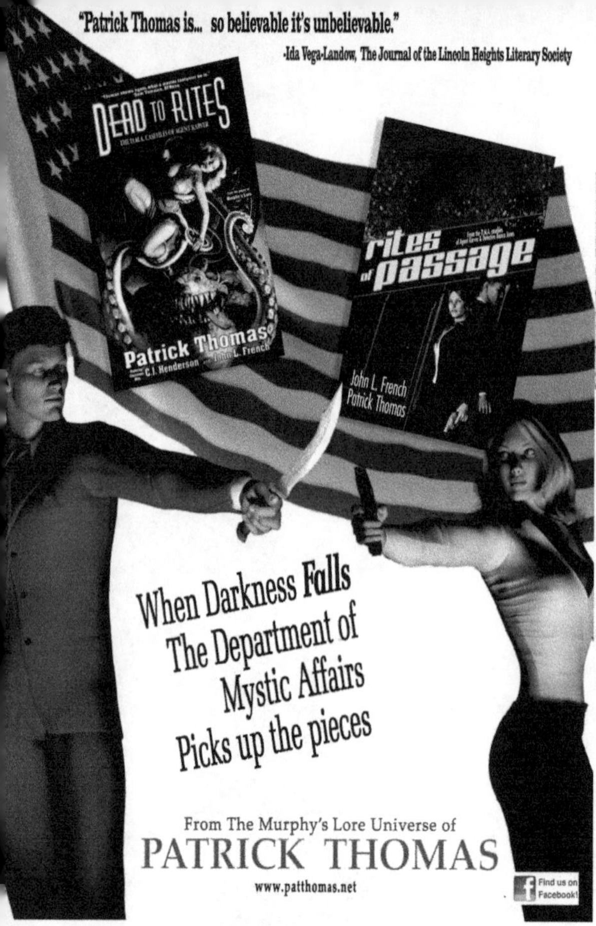

"Patrick Thomas is... so believable it's unbelievable."
-Ida Vega-Landow, The Journal of the Lincoln Heights Literary Society
Dead to Rites
Patrick Thomas
C.J. Henderson
John L. French
Rites of Passage
John L. French
Patrick Thomas
When Darkness Falls
The Department of
Mystic Affairs
Picks up the pieces
From The Murphy's Lore Universe of
PATRICK THOMAS
www.patthomas.net
Find us on Facebook!

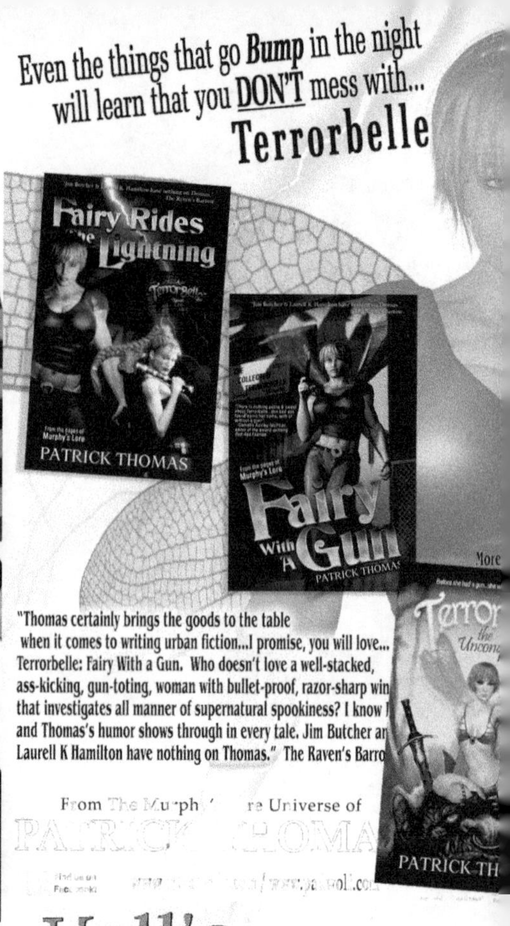

Even the things that go Bump in the night
will learn that you DON'T mess with...
Terrorbelle
Fairy Rides the Lightning
From the pages of Murphy's Lore
PATRICK THOMAS
Fairy With A Gun
PATRICK THOMAS
More
"Thomas certainly brings the goods to the table
when it comes to writing urban fiction...I promise, you will love...
Terrorbelle: Fairy With a Gun. Who doesn't love a well-stacked,
ass-kicking, gun-toting, woman with bullet-proof, razor-sharp win
that investigates all manner of supernatural spookiness? I know I
and Thomas's humor shows through in every tale. Jim Butcher an
Laurell K Hamilton have nothing on Thomas." The Raven's Barro
PATRICK THOMAS

Shape up...
You only get
ONE Warning
By Invocation Only
PATRICK THOMAS
By Darkness Cursed
Hex marks the spot
PATRICK THOMAS

Hell's Detective
No One Is Above The L
Even In
Lore & Dysorder
PATRICK THOMAS
Shadows & Brimstone
Patrick Thomas & John L. French
Case of the Moon Maniac
"Dark... and charming."
- Ellen Datow,
The Best Horror of the Year Vol. 4
"Gritty, snappy, very dark

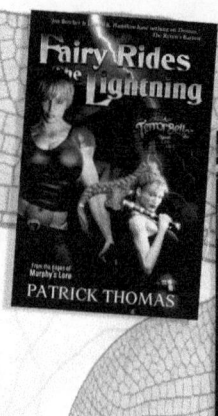

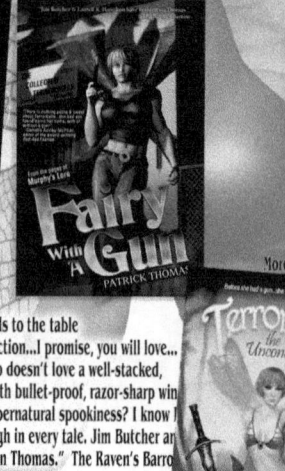

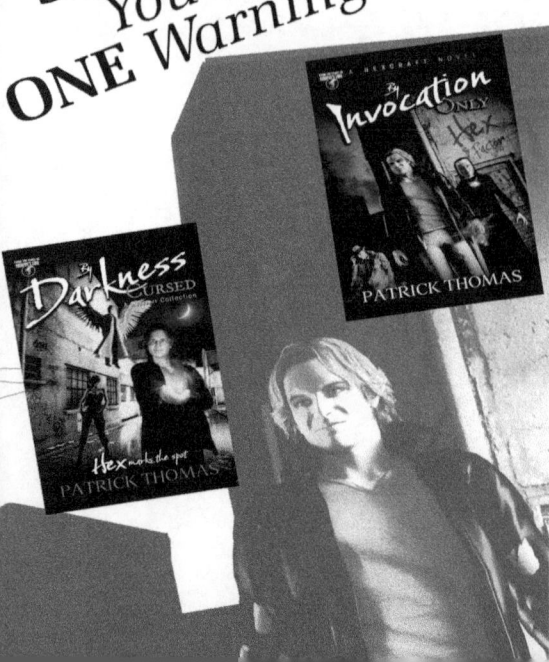

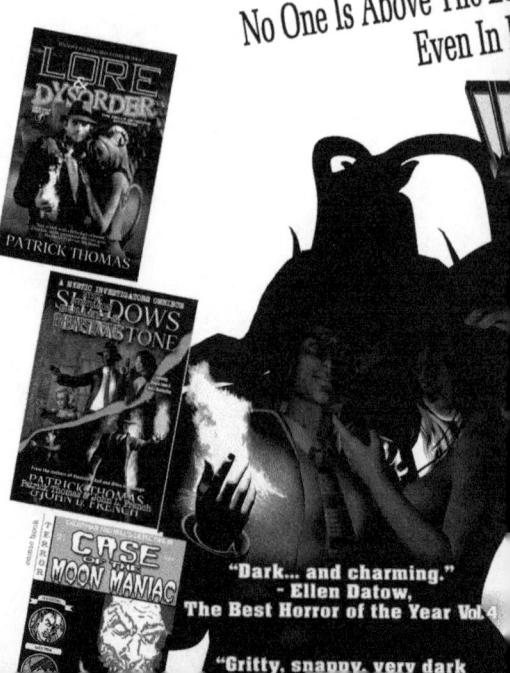

9 781890 096908